INVESTIGARE
HIDE AND SEEK

HAMILTON SPIERS

ABOUT THE AUTHOR

Hamilton Spiers was born in Belfast, Northern Ireland, where his formative years were spent during the civil disturbances of what was known as the "Troubles." He joined the Army in the 1970s and served with the Royal Irish Rangers before completing selection for a special intelligence operations unit. A career spanning over 35 years, he served in Berlin during the "Cold War" conducting intelligence gathering missions behind the iron curtain of east Berlin. He had seen service in Bosnia as a human intelligence specialist. On leaving the armed forces, Hamilton Spiers worked in Afghanistan as a Counter-Intelligence Adviser as part of "Resolute Support" in a capacity building role for US government initiatives.

During his distinguished military career, he was recognised for his service with the award of the Member of British Empire Medal (MBE) and the Queen's Commendation for Bravery (QCB). Now retired, he enjoys writing and playing golf.

Gratitude

Thanks must go to my wonderful family and my amazing wife for their help and encouragement on this incredible journey. I could not have done it without you.

Investigare

**Copyright @ 2023 Hamilton Spiers
All rights reserved**

This is a work of fiction. Names, characters, businesses, places, events, and incidents are either the product of the author's imagination or used in a fictitious manner. Any resemblance to actual persons, living or dead, or actual events, is purely coincidental. Real names and locations have only been used in cases of known historical fact, supported by independent, publicly available material.

"The views and opinions expressed are those of the author alone and should not be taken to represent those of his Majesty's Government, MOD, HM Armed Forces or any government agency."

Table of Contents

Chapter 01 – In the Beginning	07
Chapter 02 – Operation Backfire	19
Chapter 03 Sammy	50
Chapter 04 – Relocation	55
Chapter 05 – Marie's Release	60
Chapter 06 – The Funeral	75
Chapter 07 – The Meeting	87
Chapter 08 – The Stranger	91
Chapter 09 – Birthday Treat	103
Chapter 10 – The Hunt	106
Chapter 11 – Doctors Orders	114
Chapter 12 – Deception	116
Chapter 13 – Razor	125
Chapter 14 – Declan's Fixation	136
Chapter 15 – Secret Liaisons	142
Chapter 16 – Marie's Nightly Excursions	146
Chapter 17 – Tig	152
Chapter 18 – Band of Brothers	157
Chapter 19 – Operation Phone Hack	163
Chapter 20 – The Stranger	171
Chapter 21 –Follow the beetle	177
Chapter 22 - Holiday cut Short	182
Chapter 23 - The Cry for Help	191
Chapter 24 – I Can't Forget	194
Chapter 25 - Ruben	203
Chapter 26 – Operation Quick Fix	209
Chapter 27 – The Power Struggle	215
Chapter 28 – Family Business	217
Chapter 29 - Fear and Suspicion	222
Chapter 30 – The Take-away	226
Chapter 31 – The End Game	236
Chapter 32 – The Walk In	255
Chapter 33 – New Beginnings	265
Chapter 34 – Some Months Later	268
Epilogue	271

References:

CHIS. Covert Human Intelligence Agent
FRU. Force Research Unit
Hardcase. Secure Military Location
INLA. Irish National Liberation Army
IO. Intelligence Officer
OO. Operations Officer
PAC. Provisional Army Council
PIRA. Provisional Irish Republican Army
QRF. Quick Reaction Force
RUC. Royal Ulster Constabulary
SB. Special Branch
Zulu. Code word for Agent or Target
Box. Security Service or MI5
HMSU. Headquarters Mobile Support Unit
IRSP. Irish Republican Socialist Party
CID. Criminal Investigation Department
SIO. Senior Investigation Officer
DC. Detective Constable
DS. Detective Sergeant
E4. Security Service Surveillance Team
E4a. Special Branch Surveillance Team
TCG. Technical Coordination Group
DDT. Deep Dive Technology

Chapter 1

In The Beginning

Steven Tierney had numerous near compromising experiences during his time as an informer, but there was one operation he struggled to get over. Declan O'Hara had tasked him to assist "Scrappy McFarland" the head of the internal security team of the IRA which was better known as the "Nutting Squad."

Following Steven's green booking, (recruitment) by the IRA, he was deemed trustworthy by Declan. This was a huge step forward for Steven's access into the terrorist organisation and something which Sammy Carson his Special Branch handler was delighted to see. It had taken a considerable amount of time to get Steven that level of access by gaining Declan's trust.

On several occasions, Steven had been requested by Declan to collect individuals from various parts of the city and transport them to certain so-called safe houses. Declan would always be at the properties to await the arrival of these individuals. Another person who always seemed to be present was Scrappy.

Steven was under no illusions as to the nature of these meetings and the subsequent punishment being administered. It always amazed him how calm these individuals were, or at least how they managed to appear calm, knowingly, and willingly complying with their instruction to attend a meeting because of their anti-social behaviour.

Some lads were even accompanied by family members to plead their case for clemency in the hope of getting downgraded from what Scrappy called a 'Six Pack,' meaning two bullets to the knees, ankles, and elbows.

Unfortunately, Steven was seldom given notice but was expected to deliver these individuals within a quick time frame. The meetings were always quick affairs with the individuals being told the level of punishment to be administered and a location to go to for the implementation of that ruling. Steven would always at the earliest convenience relay this information to his handler Sammy. However, the punishments were always so quick in their execution, making it difficult to do anything reactive to combat it.

Declan had summoned Steven and confided in him about the growing fear within the IRA that there was a tout, (informer) within their ranks, not realising Steven had been instrumental in the arrest of one and the death of another two IRA volunteers.

'Listen Steven, Scrappy is determined to seek out whoever the tout is and "Nutt" him. Due to our recent losses everyone is under suspicion now. I need you to drive Scrappy down to Armagh this afternoon. Scrappy has business to do with a certain individual, and his guys are already in Armagh so he needs a trustworthy volunteer.

***

Steven informed Sammy of the intended trip to Armagh but stated he wasn't given a location by Declan, only a time to pick up Scrappy. When he arrived at Scrappy's house just after five in the evening he didn't go into the house; instead, he sat in the car waiting for Scrappy to exit. Scrappy acknowledged Steven through the window, only raising his hand to confirm his existence.

Several minutes later, Scrappy exited the house wearing a paddy cap, brown Barbour jacket, and blue jeans, carrying a small plastic bag. Scrappy got into the car and placed the bag into his footwell between his feet. He then spoke for the first time and asked.

'Steven I need you to stop at the corner shop, as I need cigarettes,' being his only form of interaction. When Scrappy was out of the car, Steven looked in the plastic bag and was bewildered by the presence of an old Trophy CR20 tape recorder machine and several cassettes.

Once out on the M1 motorway, Scrappy told Steven to head in the direction of the A1. After twenty miles or so, he told him to take the exit to Jonesborough. At no stage was Steven given any other instructions, despite asking where he was going.

Scrappy stated, 'You will find out soon enough just keep driving.'

Sammy had told Steven to keep him informed as to who Scrappy was meeting and if possible check in with the office. Steven was starting to get worried and considering all the previous revelations concerning the theory of a tout in their mist, he now felt he had cause for concern.

Scrappy smoked a few cigarettes during the journey, despite Steven requesting he not smoke in his car. What made it worse was the fact he smoked Camel, a non-filtered cigarette with a pungent odour. As they approached Jonesborough, Scrappy asked Steven to pull over into the entrance of the chapel just short of the village.

'I need to make a call,' said Scrappy.

Steven turned off the engine to enable him to eavesdrop and could hear Scrappy speaking to someone on the other end of the phone. Steven heard Scrappy say, 'Finbar, that's us at the village now.' Scrappy seemed to listen and then said, 'OK see you shortly.'

Scrappy got back into the car and gave Steven directions to a garage just west of Jonesborough village. Steven could just make out the lights of the village behind him. The country road was dark and uninviting as the darkness engulfed the landscape. They waited at the garage for several minutes, with Steven's anxiety levels starting to reach fever pitch.

A dark Range Rover appeared from the blackness of the night. Steven noted that the Rover had come from just over the border with the Irish Republic. The Rover never stopped in the garage but crossed the front of Steven's car, with Scrappy instructing Steven to follow it.

They travelled deep into the countryside and what seemed far from civilisation before arriving at a secluded single-story cottage with two small outbuildings.

Cathal's combi van was parked in the yard of the cottage, and this only added to Steven's anxiety. Cathal was one of Scrappy's henchmen and steven knew he would always be involved in dishing out summary justice. It was not good if Cathal and Scrappy were in the same place at the same time. It was a coming together or reunion that could only spell trouble.

Steven having parked his car in the yard was addressed by Scrappy.

'Steven go into the cottage and wait in the kitchen for me.' Scrappy then retrieved the plastic bag from the footwell and walked in the direction of an outbuilding.

The cottage was old and dated, as if an elderly person or persons lived there. There was no one else in the kitchen, but Steven could hear weak or low voices from a room to the rear of the property. Steven's mouth was dry and he felt clammy; he put his hand out straight in front of his body and it was shaking. He went over to the sink to get a glass of water, unsure of what lay ahead of him.

Steven always conscious he was working as an informer for Special Branch and the fear of compromise always present. As he was filling the glass, he continued to take in his surroundings. He could see empty sandwich packaging and a flask on the table, but his eyes were drawn to the top of the cooker. Steven thought he was looking at charred pieces of food stuck to the rings but what was odd, he could see writing, it was barely visible on one small, charred piece. As he looked closer, he could just make out what he thought were the letters L O V.

Steven dropped his glass and fell backwards, just managing to retain his balance by grabbing the edge of the kitchen table. He realised, he was looking at skin and what must have been part of someone's tattoo.

Christ, someone was being tortured here and Scrappy and Co are the masters of ceremony, he thought.

Steven felt sick to the pit of his stomach, but the sudden realisation that at least it wasn't him who was being viciously abused was almost comforting. He wanted none of it and desperately wanted to get as far away from the cottage and as quickly as possible, but he knew Scrappy would never allow him to leave now. He wasn't even sure he could find his way back out to the main roads. If only he could make a call to the office and let Sammy know what was happening but then he knew he would be mixed up in whatever dirty and treacherous deed was being carried out at the cottage.

Christ, how could I even let Sammy know where I am when I don't know myself, he thought.

Being in the Republic of Ireland further complicated the situation. Even if it had been Steven being tortured, the Police, British Army or Sammy couldn't have turned up. Steven searched the kitchen for any signs of evidence as to the location of the cottage. On the wall next to a larder cupboard was a letter rack. The rack had a small calendar with a religious picture of the virgin Mary cradling a baby. The small rack contained a set of keys and a series of envelopes. The address of the cottage was on an unopened letter from Electric I.E, the Republics main energy supplier. There was no number but rather the name Donnelly, the cottage name, 'O' Morn Cottage,' and the townland Faughart, Dundalk. The name wasn't lost on Steven as he remembered John Wayne and Maureen O'Hara in the "Quiet Man" and the cottage which had the same name.

***

Scrappy entered the outbuilding along with Finbar and was greeted by Cathal, who were in the process of dragging a male in his 30's onto a stool. The man was already in a terrible state, both physically and mentally. He was stripped down to his badly stained underwear, which were covered in wet urine stains and mud. He had horrendous burns to his legs and backside. One of his eyes was completely closed shut, with dark swelling around it. His left forearm looked like a piece of raw meat.

The man was finished, he had nothing left to give as his body and spirit were brutally broken. His dark hair was badly matted with congealed blood.

Scrappy walked to a small table and placed down the tape recorder. He then lifted a cheese slice, which had a large piece of skin still attached to it and walked over to the man, dangling it in front of his face.

'Malachy, do you know what this is? It's that pretty tattoo you had on your arm. I am going to send it in an envelope to your ma and da, you fucking tout.'

The man just moaned and pleaded through broken teeth with his torturers to stop as he had confessed already and just wanted it to stop.

Scrappy stated that was why he was there and he wanted the man to repeat all that he had told Finbar about his work with Special Branch. Scrappy then retrieved the tape recorder and Malachy told his story to Scrappy for the benefit of the tape.

***

Steven tiptoed along the corridor to the rear of the cottage before pausing outside the room he believed the voices were coming from. It sounded like two people talking in low voices in the hope of not being overheard. He opened the door slightly and peered inside and could see an elderly man and woman sitting on the side of the bed with their backs to the door. Steven quietly closed the door and retreated to the kitchen. *The elderly couple must have been placed in the room and instructed not to move, effectively being held hostage whilst the torture in the outbuildings was being conducted*, Steven thought.

Steven searched the cottage in the hope of locating a telephone, but there was none at the property, or at least none that he could find. He was in the cottage for about an hour before Scrappy and his cronies returned inside.

After a brief conversation between Scrappy and Finbar, they then made their way to the vehicles, with Steven in tow but leaving Cathal in situ.

Scrappy was in exceedingly high spirits and was extremely talkative on the route back across the border but never mentioned anything about his actions at the cottage.

Steven turned to Scrappy and asked, 'Who's Finbar?'

'Just a bloke from Armagh and someone you should forget,' Scrappy said and wouldn't be drawn any further on the matter. Steven only stated that the whole evening had been bizarre, but he was grateful to be heading home.

After dropping off Scrappy at his house, Steven went immediately to a phone box and telephoned Sammy. The location of the cottage, the people involved, and as much as he could remember was given. Steven stated that he believed a punishment beating or worse was taking place at the cottage and Cathal Conway was still in situ when he left.

Following the call from Steven, Sammy contacted his boss and was told to inform the duty commander at TCG (S) then produce an Intelligence Report detailing the information gained from Steven. The report was quickly disseminated to Special Branch for the South Armagh Region. The cooperation between the North and South policing bodies was haphazard at best, and since it was in the Garda Siochana jurisdiction, it would be their rescue operation to be conducted.

In the early hours of the morning, the Garda ERU (Emergency Response Unit), the equivalent to the British SAS managed to locate the cottage but the place was in darkness with no sign of life. On entering the cottage, they located the old man and woman, who were sitting in complete darkness on the side of the bed with their backs to the door. Both were in a state of shock and hadn't dared moved from their position in the room.

Cathal had conducted a clean-up of the property with the cooker having its rings cleaned for what was probably the first time in their existence. The outbuildings were forensically searched. Tyre casts and prints were taken, along with a non-filtered cigarette ending found at the side of the outbuilding. It was a quick response by the Garda but unfortunately didn't produce the desired outcome.

The following morning a body was found on an isolated country road on the border between south Armagh and the Republic. The body was bound, blindfolded, and had two bullet holes to the back of the head. A ten-pound note was placed in the hands of the man. It was his final payment in this life and what he was believed to be worth to the IRA for his information.

The man was later identified as Malachy Tweed, a father of three from the Armagh area.

Steven woke up to the news of the killing and was physically sick. He started to think about self-preservation. He remembered having touched the glass which dropped and broke before placing the pieces in the bin. He also touched the envelope with the address of the cottage.

God almighty, he thought, *the door handle, the table I gripped when losing balance, is there anything I didn't touch? How could I have been so stupid, now I'm implicated in a murder.*

The telephone in the secure booth of Sammy's operation room rang, making everyone in the room go silent and turn their attention to the booth. These were the dedicated telephone lines for the Agents. The Duty operator entered the booth, closing the door behind him, making it secure and silent. He picked up the phone and, after a brief moment, indicated to Sammy that it was for him.

'Hello Steven,' said Sammy, but before he had even finished a terrified Steven interrupted him but wasn't making much sense. He was rambling, and Sammy was straining to make him out.

'I'm finished, I'm finished.' Shouted Steven down the phone.

'Right slow down Steven, take a breath,' I can't help you if you are going to keep shouting at me.' said Sammy.

Steven took a deep breath and stopped talking for a moment.

'That's better. Now what's up? asked Sammy being a little more in control of the situation now.

'I'm implicated in that murder,' he insisted. The level of anxiety very much evident in his voice.

Sammy responded, 'You are not in any danger of compromise or incriminated with this murder. Let me reassure you, you did everything in your power to warn me by placing the telephone call. Malachy Tweed would have still been alive at the time of that call. The Garda were just not quick enough to avoid the subsequent move and murder from the cottage. The fact that you notified us of its location and the people present enabled us to mount the rescue operation for Malachy in the first place. Everything that could be done was done.'

Sammy spent several minutes on the phone reassuring Steven but was conscious of the time his Agent was spending on the phone, so reminded him of his personal security and the need to continue to be vigilant. Steven having got the reassurance needed, ended the call slightly less anxious than when he had started it.

However, he couldn't get his head around how Scrappy was so relaxed or unfazed by his actions. A man and a father of three was executed, and Scrappy took it all in his stride. In Steven's eyes, Scrappy and Declan for that matter were callous monsters and needed to be dealt with.

Chapter 2

Operation Backfire

Several Years Later

1:50 pm Ops Day

Rupert arrived in the carpark having received clearance from his cover teams. The call coming through his bean sized covert earpiece. The commander of the undercover police team (HMSU) had reported the arrival of Barry Nichols in the carpark as they continued their observation of him seated in his black Astra. Rupert parked alongside the Agent's Astra and indicated for the Agent to transfer into the passenger seat of his car.

Nichols, looking extremely nervous climbed in as instructed. Immediately Rupert could see Barry was on edge. He was constantly looking around as if expecting to see someone approach.

Rupert was sitting with his pistol on his lap pointing it at Nichols as he took his seat. It was clear by the look on Barry's face that he was shocked by the appearance of the pistol.

'It's not what you expected Barry, is it?' said Rupert.

Barry's eyes darted around the car, sweat beading on his forehead. He struggled to find the right words, his voice cracking under the pressure.

'I.. I don't know what you're talking about,' Barry stuttered, his voice revealing his mounting fear.

'Your little game is up my friend; your friends are probably already in the back of a police wagon.'

'I don't know what...' Barry tried to say before being interrupted.

'Stop the charade Barry, I know about the attack,' but what I don't understand is why you have done it.'

'I didn't have a choice; they were going to Nutt me for stealing from them.' Barry shifted in his seat trying to calm his shaking hands.

'You could have come to me and I would have protected you,' said Rupert. 'Haven't I always done right by you?' Rupert stopped abruptly as his earpiece burst into life in his ear.

'Standby, Standby,' came the call from the spotter on the roof of the water tower. The spotter had heard the noise of the over revved engines from the two quad bikes to the rear of his position. He had been watching the approach road into the park but not the coastal paths. On turning around, he could see the two quad bikes exiting the coastal path and approach the carpark across the open grassed area from the beach direction.

Two quad bikes with four armed assailants were closing in on the carpark. Declan O'Hara the terrorists gang leader and Mo Flynn were on one bike with Peter Rankin and John Barr the other. Each of the two teams were looking for the Astra knowing the handlers' car would be positioned next to it.

Declan had decided it was to be a full-frontal assault with Declan and Mo taking out Rupert and Barry as the second team provided protection against what he believed would be the MI5 close protection teams.

The initial radio call from the spotter had taken the heavily armed undercover police team by surprise.

"The balloon had gone up," an expression often used by the team.

On receipt of the Standby call, followed by the description of the quad bikes and the direction of attack, the two cars of the HMSU rapidly moved down the road to engage the threat.

The direction from which the quad bikes had come was certainly not expected. No battle plan survives first contact with the enemy. It was always a case of adopt and overcome.

Barry on seeing the quad bikes approaching the vehicle realised that it was no abduction, not on the back of quad bikes, The reality of the situation hit him, *I'm dead,* thought Barry.

Barry had been told the handler would be pulled out of the car and abducted before being taken away for interrogation and subsequent execution.

With his heart pounding in his chest like a Lambeg drum and sweat running down his back, Barry was desperate to escape from the car but as he reached with clammy hands for the door handle, Rupert hit the central locking button and without looking toward Barry stated,

'We're in this together, you made your bed now lie in it.'

There was a look of absolute horror on the face of Barry as he succumbed to the reality that there was no escape and the comprehension that Declan had double crossed him in his bid to kill the British spymaster along with his tout.

Rupert's adrenaline was at fever pitch as he raised his pistol in the direction of the windscreen waiting for his would-be assassins to appear but knew his life was very much dependant on the HMSU assault team and the close protection team's reaction, which he knew needed to be swift. He released the safety catch on his pistol and waited.

***

Declan steered his quad bike across the front of Rupert's vehicle. Mo as the passenger on the bike opened fire with the AK47 assault rifle, spraying the front of the vehicle with rounds. The windscreen give way to the tiny starburst shapes as the rounds penetrated the interior of the vehicle. The firing was indiscriminate with the intention of ensuring absolute carnage and death to the occupants.

Barry screamed 'Holy Mother' at the sight of the quad bike and the helmeted assassin as he still tried in vain to open the locked door by pulling on the handle and pushing with his shoulder. The first of the rounds hit him in the chest, the impact catapulting him back in his seat. He set frozen; time seemed to stand still as if he was having an out of body experience. He could see Rupert yelling as he returned fire at the attackers. Ejected casings from the pistol seemed to float past his face, then nothing but blackness and the image of his mother with her outstretched arms reaching out to him.

The two vehicles of the HMSU came to a grinding halt in the centre of the carpark. The officers alighting from the vehicles and rushing in the direction of Rupert and the quad bike assassins.

The close protection teams were already out of their vehicle and had engaged the terrorists on the second of the two quad bikes, opening fire, hitting, and killing the driver Peter Rankin who lost control of the quad toppling it upside down on the ground. John Barr was thrown clear of the vehicle and tried desperately to regain his feet running the short distance toward the wooded area to the rear of the carpark.

Having just made it to the edge of the woods, Barr was challenged by one of the plain clothed officers who had been hidden from view to the carpark. Barr, tried to raise his AK in the direction of the officer who shouted a warning before firing two rounds hitting Barr squarely in the chest, killing him instantly.

Declan having dismounted the quad bike was already in the process of approaching the front of the car with the intention of emptying his 13-round magazine into the vehicle ensuring both occupants were killed, but before he had the chance, he was challenged by members of the HMSU team.

Mo was first to turn in the direction of the advancing armed officers with their weapons trained on him. He was engaged with a rapid burst of fire neutralising him.

Declan knew the game was up and could see both occupants of the car had been hit. With his back to the advancing officers, he immediately dropped the pistol on the ground and sank to his knees with his hands in the air. His mind racing and seeing the carnage that had taken place around him, he knew the game was up. But it shouldn't have ended this way, *someone touted he* decided.

The close protection team ran to the car to check on Rupert and Barry. Rupert had been hit in the shoulder but otherwise had miraculously avoided the burst of eight rounds that had entered the car through the windscreen, one of which had penetrated his headrest.

Barry was not so fortunate as he had been shot in the chest and head. The shot to the head was like a "Bindi" red spot associated with Hindu women's tradition, worn in the centre of the forehead for spiritual beliefs that through the dot, one could seek their inner wisdom. Unfortunately for Barry whatever wisdom that had been in his brain was now splattered over his headrest and back seat with a large gaping hole in the back of his head.

Rupert was conscious but was slowly going into a state of shock. He was rambling incoherently, not really making any sense. This had been his first live contact and would later remark that everything seemed to happen in slow motion but he still had the clarity and level of focus and concentration which had become second nature following the hundreds of hours of training. It was only after the attack that the shock really hit him. His colleagues later would joke about it, stating, 'Not making sense was normal for Rupert.'

The scene had been secured by members of the HMSU team with three members of the death squad killed and Declan O'Hara arrested and taken into custody.

***

24 Hours Earlier Pre-operation

Steven Tierney a Special Branch Agent had been working undercover against the IRA for several years. He had been part of the IRA operation to kill the republican drug dealer and IRA activist, Barry Nichols.

Nichols was a double Agent. As well as being an IRA activist he was also an Agent for MI5. It was the IRA's intention to mount the operation to kill Nichols along with his MI5 handler.

Despite both the police and MI5 having undercover Agents within the IRA, none of these Agents could provide substantial information as to who the intended target was or exactly when the attack would take place.

The closest Agent to the operation was Steven Tierney who tried to warn his handler Sammy Carson of the IRA's intention to kill an informer in the coming days. The only information Steven was privy to at the time, being it was to take place when the "Tout" met with his handler.

Despite the best-efforts from Steven, he was unable to identify the target at that stage.

The IRA and in particular the Active Service Unit were keeping the details of the operation remarkably close to their chests, with only those directly involved knowing the essential details of the planned operation. It was operational procedure for each person involved only to be aware of their own involvement to prevent the risk of compromise to the overall operation. O'Hara had obtained the blessing from the Provisional Army Council (PAC) for the operation to go ahead.

Both Special Branch and MI5 took the warning very seriously but without knowing the exact details of the intended target, they felt the only options open to them was to either cancel all pre-planned operations for the foreseeable future and therefore deny the IRA a target. Alternately, they could increase the handling team's manpower attached to each operation for additional protection. The latter being decided upon. The decision was taken because of the need for intelligence in the fight against the terrorists and criminal groupings taking priority.

Nichols was known to drive himself to a designated meeting point where he would be met by his handler. Nichols had been questioned by the internal security team of the IRA and confessed to being an informer. With a subsequent promise of amnesty for his crimes by O'Hara, he had agreed to set up his handler. When questioned by the team about the Modus Operandi for the meetings, he stated that at least one, possibly two vehicles would be involved at the static meeting point. Although he had stated to his interrogators he could never positively identify any other members of the MI5 team, but he was sure they were there in the background watching.

***

Steven had been met by his handler Sammy prior to the ASU meeting taking place, but it was also before he knew the full extent of what part he would be playing in the operation.

'I've been told by Declan O'Hara I'm on standby for an upcoming attack.' Steven knew he was preaching to the converted but continued, 'O'Hara is the commander of the ASU and someone not to mess with. You know he is ruthless and wouldn't think twice about putting a bullet in the back of your head.'

News of the intended attack was pushed up the Special Branch chain of command, informing them of the pending IRA operation by Sammy. He knew the information was good grade as Steven had always provided good exploitable intelligence. He had been a confident and diligent Agent, who had been instrumental in the prevention of many previous attempted attacks against off duty police and prison officers.

One such intervention to thwart an attack occurred whilst he was conducting his taxi business around the city.

Having just dropped a fare on the Malone Road in south Belfast, he was starting to return to the city centre when he noticed a familiar Ford Escort parked at the bottom of Malone Avenue.

By manoeuvring his vehicle, he came back around but did so along an adjacent street. He saw two members of the IRA who he recognised as part of the local Active Service Unit (ASU), Paddy Court, and Freddie Gleeson. They were walking slowly in the direction of the Lisburn Road.

It didn't seem right to Steven, as they were walking away from their vehicle within an affluent residential area, which was considered neither loyalist nor republican. Both men were dressed in dark clothing, it was obvious to Steven they were up to no good.

It was later collaborated by other police and military informants that it was an ongoing targeting operation of a Special Branch officer living in the street, Ken Stones.

Micky Finn was the designated driver of the vehicle along with the two assassins. Micky had been directed to the area of Marlborough Park, off the Malone Road. He was told to wait in the car as the two men went to conduct a walk pass of the targets house to ensure the policeman's car was parked as expected. They were armed with a pistol each, having left an AK-47 assault rifle and an UVIED in the car.

As they entered the street of rich red brick, double bay, Victorian houses with their wrap-around gardens set back from the tree-lined avenue, it was unnervingly quiet. There appeared to be fewer cars parked on the street than when they had conducted the initial recce of the target's address.

Paddy noticed a dark-coloured Ford Sedan parked at the far side of the street, and the hairs on his neck instantly stood on end. He sensed something was wrong. His mouth went dry and as he went to speak to Freddie, he could not find his voice, with only a dry husky sound escaping, unable to form any words. He noticed the light above the front door of the target's house was off. This was something else that was out of place.

Lights suddenly appeared from both directions in the form of the headlights from the dark-coloured Sedan parked at the end of the street and a further vehicle which had been backed into a driveway of an adjacent property. Both men were trapped like rabbits in the headlights. It was as if the whole street had burst into life, the curtain going up in the opera house.

Suddenly, there was a shout of 'Police Stand still!'

Paddy, as if by instinct, reached for his pistol as Freddie tried to turn and run, but both men's movements were met by bursts of gunfire. Paddy was hit twice in the chest and was thrown backwards, only being stopped by a garden wall which he slid down, his body slumped against it with his chin coming to rest on his chest. Freddie was hit in the shoulder blade, the bullet entering and ricocheting up before exiting through the top of his head. Another round went through his cheekbone before embedding itself within his skull.

Micky could hear the commotion and the gunshots and immediately sought self-preservation and the need to get as far away from the incident as quickly as possible. As soon as he pulled away from the kerb, two police wagons blocked off his escape route. Suddenly there were armed police surrounding the car. Micky offered no resistance and was arrested at the scene. He was taken to Castlereagh, the police interrogation suite.

Investigare

Recovered from the car was an UVIED and an AK-47 in the backseat. Micky Finn was charged with possession of arms and ammunition with intent to endanger life. He received fourteen years, expected to serve at least ten but thanks to the GFA (Good Friday Agreement) he only served three years.

9:00 am Ops Day

Steven had just come downstairs from having a shower when his house phone rang.

'Hi Steven, it's Declan here, I need you to come to the Glen Road, the boys are already there. That wee job we talked about is on.'

Steven got dressed and left the house making his way to the address Declan had given him. On arrival at the property Steven was let into the house by the owner. A lady in her thirties who was still in her dressing gown which had seen better days and certainly never the inside of a washing machine. *She couldn't have been any older than thirty but certainly looked very much older. She appeared in his mind's eye as high as a kite from drugs.* Steven noted, when she spoke, she did so by slurring her words whilst pointing him in the direction of the kitchen door.

'They're in the back son,' she said, like she was talking to a school child.

He watched as she returned to the lounge closing the door behind her. As he walked along the hallway toward the kitchen, he could hear laughter from whoever was within. He had the sudden feeling of apprehension. His hands were clammy, so he wiped them on his jeans before reaching for the handle of the door. A knot formed in the pit of his stomach.

On opening the kitchen door, he was hit by a cloud of smoke emanating from the room of smokers stopping him in his tracks as he tried to wave away the attacking smoke, this was done more for a show of disapproval. Taking in his surrounding, he could see there were five people present who Steven believed made up the ASU team. Mo Flynn, John Barr, Barry Nichols, Peter Rankin, and the main man Declan O'Hara.

The men were seated around the kitchen table with only O'Hara standing with his back to the kitchen sink which was full of dirty pots and dishes. The room stank from the smell of tobacco.

All those present were in a fit of laughter except Barry who looked subdued to Steven. Steven wasn't sure if Barry or himself was the butt of the joke.

'What's so funny?' asked Steven,' but it was Mo who responded to him and asked, 'Steven, would you ever name your son Rupert?' before bursting out laughing with the other members joining in.

'I still don't get it' said Steven.

'Forget it,' said Declan, it's not important, but still laughing himself.

'Typical brits,' said Mo.

'OK, enough guys, let's get down to business,' said Declan. He then turned to Steven and stated, 'You've come to the party late Steven, but I need you to be the driver on this one. I need you to drop the team off and then pick us up again.'

Yet again, another surge of nervousness hit Steven. Whether it was the way Declan was looking at him or the realisation he was going to be involved in the operation, he wasn't sure but regardless of the reason he felt slightly nauseous.

'Where and where,' he asked apprehensively, meaning both drop off and pickup locations.

'I will tell you soon enough, but first, I need you to go to Mitchell's garage and pick up a wee vehicle. Mitch is expecting you. Bring it back here. Now listen, timing is essential here, so don't hang around but get straight back, understand?'

'Yeah, of course,' Steven responded. Steven took a deep intake of breath as he watched as Declan turned to Barry and said, 'Away you go. Don't let me down son, you know what's at stake.' With that, a sheepish Barry Nichols left the house through the back door.

Steven turned to go toward the back door himself when Declan said, 'Steven give it ten minutes then leave through the front door. Can't have everyone leaving at the same time now can we! Besides, anyone seeing you leave will think wee Lizzy in the front room serviced you well.

It had never occurred to Steven that wee doped up Lizzy could be on the game. He found it hard to imagine anyone wanting to willingly engage in sex with wee Lizzy. *To each their own*, he thought.

10:00 am Ops Day

Once away from the house, Steven placed a telephone call to Sammy informing him of what he knew thus far.

'I don't have a lot other than those present and the location of the safe house. I'm to be the driver for this one. But I'm not any the wiser as to who it's against or where it's to take place. Once I've got it, I'll let you know,' said Steven.

Sammy asked, 'Was there anything else you think might be important?'

Steven thought for a moment before stating, 'The only thing that appeared odd, was the joke made about the name Rupert and the "Typical Brit" comment by Mo.

Steven waited for Sammy to respond who had been silent for a moment before eventually saying, 'Right that's interesting but not sure what the relevance of it is. Once you get anything more, I need you to phone me right away. Remember the smallest detail could be vital. The vehicle details and such like once known needs to be passed right away, all right Steven?' Steven agreed to do his best and hung up the phone.

***

Sammy having finished the call with Steven, came out of the secure booth within his operations room and went straight into the boss's office and warned him of the impending operation.

'Sir, it's the usual suspects from that ASU, but the name of Barry Nichols seems odd. He's not a name I have heard being associated with that lot. I've only seen limited information in some of our intelligence reports. However, the other members of the ASU are a different story as the intelligence database is full of information concerning them. I'm hoping the analyst at the headquarters might be able to shine some more light on this Nichols character,' said Sammy.

As a result of Steven's information, a threat warning was issued following a conversation between Sammy's boss and the head of Special Branch.

10:30 am Ops Day

Steven arrived at Mitchell's garage to pick up the vehicle. He had never met mitch before and was taken aback by the appearance of the wee man. Mitch was small and stumpy who Steven thought resembled Oliver Hardy complete with mini moustache but thought it was fortunate the garage had a pit, because there was no way humpty dumpty was getting under any cars to do maintenance.

Steven thought Mitch appeared extremely nervous and could see Mitch was just anxious to get rid of the vehicle as it was potentially jeopardising his business being there. As steven recalled, he didn't have much of a choice when the two men from the IRA showed up with their uncanny ability of being able to predict the future, stating his garage could burn down should he not comply with their demands.

Steven was shown into a large, corrugated shed where a white VW Combi was parked. Immediately, Steven could see the number plates had been doctored and not particularly good. Black insulation tape had been used to change the letter L to read E and the number 1 had been changed to a 4.

Steven caused the wee man even more offence when he pointed at the plates and said, 'Fucking great job, could you not have made a few plates up?

'Just get the friggin thing out of here, and make sure you get rid of it, I don't want to see it again,' said Mitch.

'I'm going nowhere until I've checked it over, don't want the bloody thing breaking down, do we,' said Steven.

Steven had clearly rubbed the wee man up the wrong way because he was poked in his chest by Mitch who stated,

'Did you see the sign above the gate as you came in? It reads, M Mitchell Mechanic. The fucking wagon is sound, now get the fucking thing out of here.'

Steven decided to have one last poke at the bear but waited until he was safely in the vehicle with the engine running. Opening the window he said, 'It's as well you call yourself a mechanic because looking at the state of those plates you're crap at art.' As he accelerated out the gates the sound of the adjustable spanner bouncing of the door made him jump.

Once clear of the garage and on route back to the safe house, Steven placed a call through to Sammy.

'I have the vehicle. I picked it up from Mitchell's garage, he's the go to man for the preparation of the vehicles for operations. It's a white VW Combi Registration EDZ3524.'

Sammy listened as Steven expressed his concern about the Op. 'This doesn't feel right, I'm worried. It's just a gut feeling but I don't mind telling you, I'm scared. I need your assurances; I will be protected whatever happens.'

Although he was still nervous but at least Steven felt better having been reassured Sammy had his back.

11:00 am Ops Day

As a result of the information received from Sammy, the Operations Centre for MI5 were informed of the intended attack on what MI5 were able to confirm and identify as one of their officers and Agent. The location of the meeting was established during the conference call between the two organisations. The MI5 officer concerned was Rupert Conan Smythe and his Agent Barry Nichols.

Sammy now knew that was the reason he hadn't recognised the name Nichols. The name of the Agent had been protected with only general reporting within the intelligence databases and reports. An added security measure so as not to highlight his actual involvement.

The meeting between Rupert and Nichols had been originally planned for 2pm that afternoon at the Crawfordsburn Country Park. The Park being selected as it was a popular and beautiful coastal park consisting of stunning sandy beaches, woodland walks and somewhere visitors could enjoy sunbathing, swimming, and even exploring some hidden caves. But more importantly, it offered a much-needed secluded area in which Rupert could conduct his debrief of the Agent.

Sammy spoke with Rupert and asked, 'have you heard anything from Nichols by way of a warning?

'No, nothing, which is extremely worrying, I have tried to contact him but he's not responding,' said Nichols.

'We can only conclude that because he was present at the house when the ASU gathered and planned their attack, then it is a clear indication it was always going to be a set up and your man Nichols is implicit in it, said Sammy.'

'I have to agree,' responded Rupert.

***

Rupert and Sammy were summoned to attend a hastily arranged meeting at Belfast's regional command centre. Once it was decided on a plan of action, it was into the Operations Room for the detail planning and orders process.

Sammy was adamant he needed to be involved as it was his Agents intelligence that had discovered the IRA's intentions to assassinate the MI5 man. He also believed at some stage during the day his Agent would get back in touch with updates and therefore it would be prudent for him to remain in the command centre.

Investigare

It was decided a covert police team (HMSU) knowing of the intended static meet location could pre deploy within the Crawfordsburn Country Park with the goal of arresting the terrorist team. The entrance to the park was being observed by undercover officers from HMSU. Two of their unmarked vehicles had been positioned within the grounds blending in with the numerous visitors to the popular venue to affect the intercept and arrest of the ASU members on receipt of a radio call.

The commander for the operation believing they could apprehend the ASU team before it had a chance to engage their intended target. Additional undercover officers were positioned in the woods providing close support to the handler's car. An additional spotter was placed on top of the large water tower which provided excellent field of view covering the whole operational area. It was agreed everyone except the MI5 handler and his deputised team would be in position for 1pm.

***

Rupert Conan Smythe had been with the Security Service for three years having been recruited straight from Oxford university following his graduation with his first-class honour's degree in English and modern history. He was a tall good looking athletic individual with sharp features and golden blond hair. He was a popular member of MI5 or as it was also known "BOX" especially with the ladies, but according to his colleagues he had the brain the size of a planet but the common sense of a gnat.

He came from a wealthy family and had two brothers. The eldest Timothy was a consultant in Harley Street whilst Oliver ran the large family estate in Hampshire. Rupert being the youngest was considered the "Spare" and as with many aristocracy families, he was destined for the military or government. Rupert opting for the government and the Security Service.

Rupert had been the primary handler for Barry Nichols since his arrival in province eighteen months previous. He hadn't done anything wrong on the case, believing the case had been progressing well with a good level of control and direction. The Agent had been producing some excellent reporting. But unknown to Rupert, it was the Agent's own activities that got him ousted. Barry had been skimming of the top from his drug bosses of the IRA. It was under interrogation that Barry had admitted to being a tout which had led to the IRA mounting of the operation.

11:30 am Ops Day

Steven received a call from O'Hara and was told he needed to pick the team up from an address on the Falls Road. As a precaution they had moved away from their earlier meeting point for fear that Barry could compromise their location. It just so happened it was to the house where the arms cache was located to be used in the operation.

On arrival at the new address, Declan briefed Steven on the next phase of the operation.

'I need you to get me and the boys to the drop off point at Carnalea Bay carpark and slipway. Once dropped, make your way to Fort Point Road.'

Steven knew this to be the most northern point of the Helens Bay coastline. It was the site of the old gun emplacements used to guard Belfast Lough during the war.

'Wait for us there, we will come to you once the attack is over. Today we get to kill a Brit handler and the tout bastard Nichols,' said Declan.

Although Steven had been present on the operational planning meeting as the driver. He was not made aware of the target until now.

Christ, Nichols, the poor bastard, no wonder he looked so subdued earlier at the house, thought Steven. It was only when he arrived at Carnalea Bay he saw the white transit van that had delivered the two quad bikes prepared and waiting for the teams intended use.

1:30 pm Ops Day

On arrival at Carnalea, the ASU exited the vehicle and removed a large black holdall from the back of the Combi. Contained inside the holdall were three AK-47's assault rifles and a 9mm browning pistol. Each of the assault rifles had two magazines of rounds taped to each other. Each magazine containing thirty rounds, this being an excessive amount of firepower to kill two men.

Each of the men were dressed in black boiler suits and a dark coloured scarf or bandana which could be pulled up over their mouth and nose. Crash helmets with large dark goggles had been placed on top of the quad bikes ready for use.

Declan took possession of the pistol then issued the other three members of the team their AK's. He then instructed Steven to go directly to Fort Point Road. This was known locally as Grey Point which was now a museum. He was told to get there and wait for the ASU's arrival.

As he started his exit from the park back toward the road, he noticed the transit van was behind him. This caused him some concern as he knew he wouldn't be able to stop to telephone Sammy. The van remained behind him all the way to Grey Point, but much to his relief it turned left on the Craigdarragh Road heading back toward the village of Holywood. Steven then continued the last few hundred meters to Grey Point. It was a natural route for the transit van to take but it just ensured Steven couldn't get access to a telephone and warn Sammy of the ASU's intentions.

Declan and the team travelled a short distance into a small wood clearing next to the coastal path to make final adjustments to their equipment and weapons for the attack. Declan a ruthless and dedicated terrorist reflected on what was about to take place. His hatred of "Touts" knowing the untold damage they have done to the IRA over the years resulting in the death of many a good volunteer because of their snitching to their Brit handlers was unpalatable to him.

There was nothing worse than a tout. Declan had worked himself up into a frenzy. He was so pumped up on adrenaline and relished this opportunity to take out the tout bastard. Having mounted the quad bikes, he give his last motivational words to the team, "Tiocfaidh ár lá" (Our day will come).

Post Operation

Steven waited for the ASU to arrive at Grey Point but having heard the gun fire in the distance and no sound of the quad bikes along the coastal pathway, he became extremely worried. His heart was pounding in his chest as he watched the minutes tick slowly by. He knew that O'Hara could easily turn on him if he suspected that he had betrayed them. As the minutes passed and not seeing any sign of the quad bikes, his anxiety continued to mount. He decided to get out of the area and as far away from the operation as possible.

***

Steven had just arrived home having disposed of the combi when the two men turned up and asked him to accompany them for a wee chat. He had been taken by them to a safe house on the Falls Road. He had been led into the house by the two men but once through the entrance they set upon him ramming his head against the wall before administrating several punches and placing a sack over his head.

He kicked and struggled against the two brutes and had given a decent account of himself but was eventually overwhelmed as he was dragged along the hall into the back room and shoved down into a chair.

He was quickly secured with plastic cuffs by the hands and legs to the chair. It all happened so fast, but then there was a total silence over the room. The sack offered no view at all, with only speckles of light cascading through, but the strong smell of a potent cigarette smoke was wafting through the fabric with ease and getting into his nostrils as he desperately tried to regulate his breathing.

The room must have been sparsely furnished because the slightest noise or movement seemed to reverberate off the walls. He recognised the sound of a tape recorder button being pressed. Then he heard a voice for the first time.

'So, here we are.' It was the voice of Cathal Conway. Cathal was now the head of the internal security team of the IRA. *Christ not again* thought Steven, having had previous experiences with the man which he liked to forget. Cathal was someone to be feared. Steven was told by him,

'You are being questioned on the grounds of being suspected as a tout and the reason for the failed operation.'

'What we have here is a tout bastard who jeopardised our operations. A traitor and brit lover who has betrayed his community, family, and fellow republicans. But before long, you will give a full confession, because if you don't, you will never see your family again. So, we can do this the easy way or the hard way, that's entirely up to you and how well you cooperate.'

The hessian sack was ripped off his head, and as he had already envisaged, the room was empty except for the chair he was seated in and a small coffee table which had a series of instruments such as pliers, a claw hammer, and even a cheese slice, all of which he immediately recognised as torture tools. If the equipment on the table were props and designed with the intention to scare him, then they certainly had the desired effect. His heart rate had increased to the extent that he thought at any moment it would pop right out of his chest.

There was a large plastic decorator's sheet covering much of the floor around the seat. He was facing the wall with 70's style retro wallpaper consisting of large yellow and green flowers. The wallpaper hurt his eyes more than the single hanging light bulb from the ceiling as his eyes adjusted to the room. Heavy, cheap, green velvet curtains were drawn closed. These were too long for the window, with the bottom of the curtain lying on the floor in a heap.

'I swear to God, I know nothing about why the operation was botched. I had nothing to do with any of this and I'm no fucking tout,' protested Steven.

'Well maybe a little persuasion might just jog your memory.' With that, Cathal nodded to one of his minders who walked over, punching him hard on the side of the jaw.

Blood splattered from his mouth, spraying the plastic sheet. He wasn't sure if he had lost any teeth with the punch, but it certainly loosened one or two. The rusty metallic taste of blood was sickening and made him feel queasy.

'Has that refreshed your memory?' asked Cathal.

His head was spinning, and trying to speak whilst spitting blood, he stated, 'I really don't know what you want me to say because I've done nothing wrong.'

They were relentless in their questioning and torture practices. He had been with his interrogators for over twenty-four hours.

Steven continued to plead his case and said, 'I didn't tell anyone, anything. Christ, I knew nothing about the Op until it took place,' he protested.

Eventually Cathal said, 'your free to go but if following our investigation, we find out that you betrayed us, there will be consequences.' Steven just nodded but was relieved. 'I understand' he said, but I never told anyone. I'm not responsible for any betrayal.' Steven continued stating, 'Others involved in the operation could have been responsible for the leak.' He tried to explain that the driver of the transit van could be responsible but was told he had already been cleared.

He then turned his attention to the dead Barry Nichols by explaining he may have confessed to his Brit handler and therefore facilitated the setup of the ambush but had just been unlucky to get wasted himself. Nothing deflected the finger of suspicion being pointed at him. Steven was left badly shaken and bruised because of what was considered a preliminary interrogation for answers.

'This was only round one,' stated Cathal. 'If you had anything to do with this Tierney, you will disappear. You will be Nutted.'

He was released but told he would be questioned again by members of the internal security team once they had a chance to speak with Declan at the Maze prison for his side of the story.

***

It came as a great relief when Steven eventually contacted Sammy. Steven was in a terrible state. With a trembling voice, Steven said, 'Sammy I'm going to be "Nutted" and I don't believe I could survive any further interrogation.' He pleaded with Sammy, 'You need to take me and my family into protective custody.'

Although he was an excellent asset and had provided valuable intelligence over the years as a confidential informant, he was becoming battle scarred and in the period leading up to the operation had shown signs of reluctance to get involved, self-preservation was steering his commitment.

This was something Sammy was very much aware off and had to agree with. The protection program is the worst-case scenario. It means the total upheaval of a family by removing them from everything that is dear to them. A family having to leave behind mothers and fathers never to see them again. It is not something to be taken lightly and Sammy knew only too well the consequences of such a drastic measure.

Sammy had already been privileged to intelligence reporting from MI5 by an Agent codename "Thornbush" that Tierney was to be the sacrificial lamb for the failed operation. Sammy and his bosses at the headquarters felt they had no option but to put in place a plan to have Steven Tierney and his family moved to the mainland with new identities. His time as an Agent for the state had run its course.

***

The Tierney family packed up their car in the early hours of the morning to leave their west Belfast home behind, knowing they could never return. Life would never be the same again. Steven struggled convincing his wife Rose that it was the only option open to them.

'Rose listen to me, I'm dead if we stay here and life would be unbearable for you and Paul.'

Their son Paul had just turned sixteen and was devastated by the news. After a torrent of abuse directed at his Dad, the lad broke down and cried non-stop. Steven did everything in his power to explain why he had become an Agent for the state in the first place, but it was falling on death ears and he was running out of time. They needed to leave and sharpish.

'I promise, one day you will understand. I have saved so many lives, fathers, mothers, sons, and daughters because of what I have done. I have saved lives not taken them, said Steven.'

Investigare

Steven watched as Rose and Paul packed. Both being confused as to what they should take. Rose couldn't believe she was having to leave all her worldly goods that she had spent her whole life collecting. This had been her Mum's house before it was passed to her following the death of her Mum. She had so many childhood memories in it. Paul was born in it and now she had to leave it all behind.

As Steven put the rest of their belongings in the back of the car, he could see Rose looking back at the house with tears flowing down her face. *What memories was she recalling,* he thought as he got back into the driving seat. As he drove away, he refused to look into the rear-view mirror, he decided it was now behind him and that is where it should remain, in the past. They must look forward to their new lives away from Northern Ireland. The family were escorted to a Safe House in the Antrim countryside where they were accommodated whilst their new identities were produced. It was here the Tierney family met their new custodians for the transition and settlement outside Northern Ireland.

***

Following the IRA operation to kill Rupert Conan Smythe and Barry Nichols, Declan O'Hara received ten years for the murder of Nichols and the attempted murder of the MI5 handler. He only served a total of three years as he was released following the GFA. On his release from prison, Declan was met at the gates of the Maze prison by Razor Fox. The first words Declan said to Razor was, 'Has there been any update on the whereabouts of that tout bastard Tierney.'

Three years had passed but his thirst for revenge had not diminished. Declan passionately believed Tierney was responsible for the death of the complete ASU. Three of his mates and comrades died that day and he wanted revenge no matter how long it would take. He continued to pursue several lines of inquiry but every avenue he went down was a dead end. No matter how hard he tried, he had been unable to locate him.

'I will continue to hunt him till my dying day,' he said to Razor. 'I have thought of nothing else over the past three years. I will get him,' he declared.

Chapter 3

Sammy

Sammy had been a Special Branch handler for over ten years with a responsibility for several undercover Agents operating within the terrorist organisations both loyalist and republican in Northern Ireland. In his time working for the police, he only ever had one Agent needing relocated under the police protection program, which was Steven Tierney.

Sammy a native of Belfast had witnessed the worst of the troubles as a young man. Having himself been involved in many a riot. He always remembered the buzz of adrenaline and excitement he got during the skirmishes with the Police and Army at the interfaces of the Shankill and Falls road.

He had a vivid memory of the banging of metal bin lids on the walls and ground by the women and kids, a tactic adopted as an early warning system for the impending arrival of the security forces in the area. This would normally be followed by the sound of the crack and thump as the paramilitaries from both sides exchanged gunfire.

There was also the unforgettable smoke-filled air that lingered over the area with its potent smell of burning rubber of tyres from the burnt-out buses used as barricades. It was a feeling like no other.

He never once contemplated what his indiscriminate throwing of bricks and bottles had on the recipients of his actions. However, many years later as a police officer he had experienced knowing exactly what it was like to be on the receiving end of such actions.

Sammy finished his schooling with good grades but took the view of wanting excitement, adventure and seeing the world. His father had worked all his days in the shipyard and he knew that he didn't want to follow in his footsteps, so found himself in Palace Barracks and the recruitment office of the Army.

Having done well in his aptitude test he knew he had a choice to make. He was offered a place at the apprentice college of the Royal Engineers (RE) or the Royal Electrical and Mechanical Engineers (REME) but opted to join the Parachute Regiment. The idea of throwing himself out of an airplane excited him. Although the recruiting officer did try and convince him to join his local Regiment "The Royal Irish Rangers" having stated, 'The jumping bit was just a short cut to the battlefield. Once on the ground you were still an Infantry soldier.'

Sammy was adamant of his choice and was sent to Aldershot in the south of England to the PARA Depot. He received a challenging time during his recruit training because of his Irish nationality. He was bullied by the senior instructors and was often in fights as if he and he alone was responsible for the Northern Ireland "Troubles" and the death of several paratroopers, but he was a resilient son of a bitch and determined to hold his own.

The Falkland's war give him more than his fair share of adrenaline rushes and adventures along with his numerous deployments back to Northern Ireland. He was recognised for his service with a Mentioned in Dispatches (MID) or better known as the Queens Commendation for Bravery.

On leaving the Army, he joined the RUC and served with distinction for the most part. He had survived numerous assassinations attempts on his life from both the loyalists and republicans alike. He would often joke that he had to relocate under threat more times than Blair International Transport moved goods.

Sammy's marriage of twenty years came to an end following the death of his son Noah. His wife suffered a complete mental breakdown and never got over the death. Their lives together following Noah's death became extremely strained with Sammy turning to the bottle and only ever finding solace in the bottom of a glass.

Roy and Davy his friends and colleagues in the police were instrumental in getting Sammy back on the straight and narrow and saving his job in the process. However, they were unable to help him salvage his marriage.

Although she never blamed Sammy for what happened but the pressures of living under the constant threat of attack had taken its toll. In many ways Sammy was happy he had separated as he felt he couldn't protect her. He had always stated that he needed to be lucky all the time but the terrorists only ever needed to get lucky once to cause carnage and death. He was of the mindset, he had failed his son and wife and had to live with that.

He would often think back to that tragic day and the duplicitous and cowardly act.

It was a routine Saturday morning and his son's schools under 15's rugby match. Noah a student at Campbell College Grammar School was a promising young rugby player. As a fly half he was light but extremely fast on his feet and never showed any fear when playing, regardless of the size of the opposition.

Sammy was proud of the lad and could see he had the same determination and grit he saw in himself.

As he was preparing to leave for the match to take Noah to his game, he carried out his usual diligent search of car and driveway. As he glanced in through the window of his VW estate he looked to see the small light of his anti-explosive device detection system. Had the light indicated red then something metallic would have been attached to the underside of the car.

The light of the device was green and he was reassured the vehicle had not been tampered with during the evening. Not a normal way of life by any standard but Northern Ireland was anything but normal at that time. A simple lapse in security could end in certain death.

IED's had been used to great effect by the terrorists causing many a death and maiming of security force personnel. IED's were often crude devices and simple in design but they could also be sophisticated, incorporating modern electronic components. These devices allowed the terrorists to strike without being decisively engaged with their target.

Sammy had always taken his own safety and that of his family's extremely serious. On that tragic morning and as he was preparing to leave, Noah had exited the house but despite having been made aware of the need to be vigilant and unknown to Sammy, Noah had seen a football at the side of the garden on the lawn. He went over thinking someone must have kicked it into the garden by accident but hadn't come to retrieve it.

As he bent to pick it up, Sammy could see him out of the corner of his eye and immediately sensed the danger. He started to shout at Noah not to touch the ball but wasn't quick enough. Noah lifted the ball and the IED exploded killing Noah instantly.

The device was indiscriminate. The evil people who planted the device showed a total disregard for human life. It mattered not who moved the ball only that someone would lose their life.

Over the years it had always been drilled into soldiers and police alike, never to touch anything whilst out on patrol for the very reason that it may be booby trapped. The incident destroyed the family. It took a long time but Sammy eventually managed to continue with his career.

Chapter 4

Relocation

Sean and his son Peter fished on the banks of the Nith river most Sundays. It was their favourite spot which was secluded and located on the outskirts of Dumfries but only a mile from their home in the village of Heathhall. The picturesque village with a population of just under 3,000 had been home to the Tierney family since their untimely move away from Northern Ireland.

Having been given new identities, the newly named Talbot family seemed happy with their new life and had settled well. The government having provided them with a new home and a small bookshop business which Sean and Peter took turns in managing. The name change took some getting used to though. But they eventually adopted to their new names over time.

Their new home was a small, detached cottage on the outskirts of the village. It needed a little bit of work and TLC but it was home and they had all the time in the world to make it better.

Having a large front and rear garden was a luxury they never had back in Belfast. It was so far removed from what the Tierney's were used too.

In the centre of the village stood a quaint, white-washed church, and its bell tower which would chime melodiously, marking the passing of time and drawing the villagers to gather for Sunday service.

The village was surrounded by rolling hills and lush meadows, where livestock grazed peacefully. Dotted throughout the landscape were pictorial farmhouses, their thatched roofs blending seamlessly into the natural beauty that enveloped them.

In the initial months following their move they were frequently visited by Sean's old handler Sammy from Special Branch; this was to help the Talbot family with the transition to their new lives. Their new identities in the form of passports, driving licences and even the credit cards were produced courtesy of the government as part of the process to help the family settle.

Rita, Sean's wife had found the transition profoundly more difficult to adjust too but this was the penance she had to endure for Sean's actions. It was the constant lies she had to tell of their fictitious existence before their life in Heathhall that she despised so much. It was hardest in the first year of their move to make new friends for fear of letting their guard down and potentially compromising themselves. Eventually they grew more accustomed to their new lives and adopted to it. There could be no atonement for what had happened, this was their future now.

You can take the girl out of Belfast but you can't take Belfast out of the girl.

Rita would occasionally get homesick as she missed the Belfast craic. She yearned to go home permanently but knew there was no hope of it ever happening. It was an idealism and not a practicality.

This was her new life now, for better or worse. She had taken her wedding vows very seriously but the move away from Belfast had put a major strain on her relationship with Sean despite having an extremely comfortable lifestyle.

If she left him, she could go home but she would still be under pressure to divulge the whereabouts of her husband. More importantly, as Sammy reminded her, she would be ostracised by her community and there was a real possibility she would be interrogated to disclose her husband's whereabouts.

Anyway, she loved him too much for that to even be an option. Although she could never understand what motivated him to work for the police as an informer. Regardless of his motive or reasons for doing what he did, he was still her husband and in her eyes not some sort of Machiavellian monster.

The upheaval affected Peter more than anyone else. It was because at the time of being relocated he was still just a teenager and had to leave all his friends behind, but whatever the reason, the first few years were hell. He had been secretly smoking cannabis and drinking alcohol despite only being sixteen years old at the time of the move.

Sean was the target of both their frustrations and happily accepted the anger directed at him. Eventually the anger and frustrations subsided, Sean was able to get Peter back on the straight and narrow. However, a lot of water had passed under the bridge since then and the family had been living and enjoying their new lives for five years.

The Sunday fishing excursions was one such event that helped. Lazy summer days lying on the picturesque banks of the river with only the sounds of birds and the flow of water cascading over the sporadically positioned rocks penetrating their ears. It was a relaxing pastime and in a lot of ways it was helping them to forge new memories. These were better memories for them away from Belfast and all that it represented.

They would spend full days in this tranquil setting not returning home until the last of the sun rays could be seen setting behind the trees and the sound of the village church bells calling the villagers to their evening service.

Accompanied only with their own thoughts, flasks of tea and sandwiches and the odd success of a catch. Competition was fierce between the two for the biggest fish. This being far removed from the stress of his double life working for the SB and the drug fuelled gangs of the paramilitaries.

The family had numerous conversations during their settling period of how dangerous it would be if they had any lapses of security. The fear of them doing something that could lead to them being compromised was primary in these discussions. It had been emphasised to the family by Sammy his ex-handler that any form of compromise or carelessness could result in death. The SB team had taken a back step believing everything that could be done for the family's welfare and safety had been achieved. It was now down to the Talbot family to make the most of their new lives.

Chapter 5

Marie's Release

Marie Coyle had served ten years of a life sentence for the murder of the IRA's head of internal security, or as it was better known the "Nutting Squad," and its leader Scrappy McFarland. It was something she never showed any remorse or regret for. Her husband had been killed on the orders of Scrappy.

Marie had told her good friend Teresa Stitt, 'He may not have pulled the trigger himself but he was just as guilty as the man who did.'

No one was ever convicted of her husband's murder, so Marie took it upon herself to seek retribution on Scrappy McFarland.

Marie's husband, Tim Coyle had been accused of being a police informer, something later denied by the police ombudsman. One of the very few acknowledgements ever made on behalf of the government. Another wrongly accused and alleged informer who the government cleared was Jean

McConville a mother of ten who was murdered at the hands of the IRA.

In the case of Tim Coyle, he had been abducted by the IRA and taken to Dundalk in county Louth, a known region predominately used by the west Belfast IRA for interrogations and executions over the years. Most suspected informers were always found with their hands bound, blindfolded with two bullet holes to the back of the head and dumped like bags of rubbish in the border area.

Tim Coyle's post-mortem revealed he had received the most horrendous of torturing. All his fingernails had been extracted with pliers causing untold excruciating pain. He had cigarette burn marks all over his torso and genitals. Hydrochloric acid had been used on his nipples and navel. His face was so savagely beaten that Marie couldn't have an open casket when his body was eventually returned to her. To add insult to injury the community turned against her for her husband's alleged actions.

The thought of revenge had consumed Marie's thoughts, overwhelming every other emotion within her. Her desire for vengeance had burned deep within her like a raging fire. She was determined to make those bastards in the IRA who had murdered her husband pay dearly for their actions. Every night, Marie had lay in bed, plotting all their downfalls and picturing how she would inflict her revenge.

With each passing day, her thirst for revenge grew stronger. It had become her sole purpose in life, ignoring any potential consequences of her actions. Marie had planned her revenge to coincide with the first anniversary of her husband's murder. Revenge had become her motivation.

Following several months of mourning, she openly started flaunting herself at Scrappy McFarland. On the night of the anniversary of Tim's death, Marie called to the house of her good friend Teresa Stitt having previously arranged to have a girl's night out at Sandy's bar for its traditional Friday night Disco.

Teresa had noted and commented to Marie that she looked like she was dressed to kill, meaning very provocatively which seemed out of character for her.

'Marie I've never seen you dressed in such a short skirt and that blouse is transparent. That's a nice, laced bra by the way. You'll knock them dead in that outfit love.'

'That's my intention,' Marie said with a chuckle.

Following a glass of wine in the house, the two girls made their way to Sandy's. On opening the door to the bar, the girls were hit with the pulsating beats of the music that filled the air, making it almost impossible to hold a conversation without shouting.

The dance floor was virtually empty with only one couple who were already drunk trying desperately to dance by gyrating their bodies, but certainly not in sync to the rhythm of the music.

The bar itself had been dimly lit to create a warm and inviting atmosphere. The barman was busy pouring pints for eager customers, their raised laughter blending with the music.

The walls of the bar were decorated with pictures of local Gaelic football teams and memorabilia of republicanism. Strobe lighting flashed periodically, enhancing the disco experience, making the crowd feel like they had stepped back in time as 70's music blasted out from the speakers.

As the night progressed, the energy in the bar intensified. The disco fever had taken hold of everyone, and the dance moves became more elaborate and daring.

Teresa fetched the two girls a drink before deciding to take a table as far away from the stage and dance floor as they could get, otherwise they would never hear each other speak over the noise of the music speakers. Within minutes, Marie notice Scrappy come from an area to the rear of the bar but no sooner had he appeared in the bar he retreated out of sight again. Her heart missed a beat; her pulse rate had increased when he first appeared as she contemplated what was to come.

Marie knew Scrappy was known for his womanising but wasn't known for being particularly choosey. When slagged by his mates about his choice of women, he would always give the same retort, 'You don't look at the mantel piece when poking the fire.'

Although even Marie knew Scrappy would have been punching well above his weight to be with her. He would be someone she would never have contemplated dating even if she were single. She was an extremely good-looking woman with long blond hair with a slim and a well-toned body with beautiful deep blue eyes.

Marie had been in Sandy's bar that evening because she knew Scrappy would be in the back room conducting IRA business. She laughed to herself knowing these back rooms were known as "Romper Rooms," named as such after a very popular children's television series in the 1970's. It was a place where games were played out.

Children would be seated in front of the television desperately trying to guess which one of three windows the story was behind. But this version was much more sinister as it was normally IRA meetings and punishment beatings and such likes that would be carried out in these rooms.

The girls were on their second drink when Scrappy returned to the bar noticing Marie and Teresa sitting drinking at a table. Marie had deliberately tried to get his attention by way of the odd glance and flirtatious smile at him. She knew IRA members wives were considered off limits at least those that were incarcerated but she didn't fit that bill, she was a widow and a tout bastards' widow at that. So, she knew she would be considered fair game.

Scrappy wasn't slow on the up take and as he approached both ladies, Marie's heart rate was racing.

'Two lovely ladies shouldn't be sitting alone,' said Scrappy.

It was Teresa who was quickest with her retort, by saying, 'But we're not alone, we're together,' as both girls laughed.

'Cute and funny. Can I get you both a drink?' asked Scrappy.

'No, we're fine,' Teresa tried to say before being interrupted by Marie who said, 'That would be great thanks.'

Teresa give Marie a look of annoyance but Marie ignored the look and watched as Scrappy walked back in the direction of the bar to get the drinks.

'You do know who he is, don't you!' said Teresa.

'Yes of course, the man is just buying us a drink, stop worrying,' said Marie.

After drinking the drink bought by Scrappy, Teresa could see how Marie seemed totally preoccupied with the attentions of Scrappy, so quietly spoke into Marie's ear saying, 'Listen Marie, I think I'll leave you to it, I feel like a "Spare" here and he clearly doesn't want me here. He's all over you like a rash.' She then warned her good friend to be careful before saying, 'I'll see you tomorrow love.'

Both girls stood and hugged with Marie holding onto Teresa extremely tightly before releasing her grip and saying, 'You're a good friend Teresa,' She then kissed her on the cheek and looking directly into her eyes she said, 'You take care love,' before releasing her grip.' Having said their goodbyes Marie rejoined her company of Scrappy McFarland.

Teresa didn't know what to make of her friends' actions, there was a mysterious look in her friends' eyes and a sadness which worried Teresa.

Teresa couldn't help but feel a sense of confusion and concern after Marie's parting words. The tight embrace, the kiss on the cheek, and the intense gaze in Marie's eyes all left Teresa with a feeling of unease. There was something deeper going on, something Teresa couldn't quite grasp.

As she walked the short distance home, lost in her thoughts, Teresa replayed their conversation in her mind. Marie had mentioned a few times that she was going through a difficult time following the death of her husband, but Teresa hadn't expected such an intense display of emotion. Their friendship had always been strong, but this was different.

Investigare

Unable to shake off her worry, Teresa decided to reach out to Marie later that night. She telephoned Marie's house but never got an answer. She couldn't shake off the feeling that something wasn't right. She left a voicemail, simply saying, 'Hey Marie, I hope you're okay. You seemed a bit off earlier. If you ever need someone to talk to, you know I'm here for you. Take care.'

***

Marie was now alone with the "Big I am" following Teresa's departure from the bar.
'Why don't we carry on our wee chat in the back room. We can have a private drink and not be disturbed,' said Scrappy. Marie just smiled at the man raising her eyebrows which could only be interpreted as a yes by Scrappy. Scrappy led Marie into the storeroom which housed the kegs, bottles and cans that supplied the bar with its beer. It was dingy and damp and smelt of stale beer.
Once alone in the storeroom, he wasted no time in pawing at her with his stumpy grubby hands and his dirty chewed fingernails. He grabbed her breast with one hand as he forced her backwards up against shelfing. His free hand went straight between her legs. *Christ he's like a man possessed,* thought Marie. Scrappy had already managed to bypass her short skirt as he reached for her crutch. She was repulsed by him and the smell of his breath from stale smoke and alcohol was almost

overpowering. Marie pushed him back away from her and lied, 'I want this as much as you do, but do you have to be so fucking rough.'

He stepped back from her and apologised, then looked around the room for a better spot to perform sex. Marie suggested it would be easier if she bent over the beer kegs as she would have something to hold onto, pointing to the far side of the room.

He smiled and turned toward the kegs whilst undoing his belt and Jeans preparing to release his penis. Whilst his back was to Marie she reached into her shoulder bag and removed the large knife. She thrust forward plunging the knife deep into his back. He let out a loud scream but the sound of the music from the bar masked his cries of anguish. She pulled the knife back to strike him again but his Celtic top had already turned an instant shade of crimson as the blood oozed out of the wound.

He fell into the Kegs banging his head on the edge of one before landing on his back on the damp floor. Scrappy just lay there looking up at Marie with a bewildered expression on his face.

As he lay there, it was obvious to her that she must have punctured his lung because he found it almost impossible to breathe. She thought to herself, *God, the bloody knife must have gone all the way through his body as it was embedded right up to the handle as she had found it difficult to get it back out.*

Marie stood astride him knife in hand and said, 'Tonight, is the anniversary of my Tim's murder and you were responsible for that murder McFarland. I promised I would get you and your cronies no matter how long it took.' She then stabbed him several times in the chest. Marie couldn't recall how many times she stabbed him but she was covered in blood. Her clothes, her face and hair was completely covered. She stood over his body and watched as he took his last breaths waiting for the wheezing to eventually stop.

She could barely remember walking back into the bar and seeing and hearing people screaming at the sight of her. At first those present believed it was Marie that was hurt but quickly realised it wasn't her as she was still holding the knife in her hand. Marie just stood there in the middle of the bar with the spinning flashing lights from the disco illuminating her.

When she thought back on it, *it must have seemed like a scene from the horror movie "Carrie" as she stood there covered in blood.* The police were called but not before many of the IRA boys disappeared from the bar. Marie was taken into custody. As far as she was concerned the bastard got what he deserved. She felt no remorse or regret, just satisfaction that justice was eventually served.

***

Teresa Stitt had travelled up to HMP Magilligan Prison. The prison was located at Northern Ireland's most northern point. She was going to pick up her good friend Marie Coyle. As Teresa arrived at the main carpark which was situated directly outside the prison main entrance and only a matter of a few hundred meters from the Magilligan Point and the Point bar and restaurant.

The area had one of the finest beaches in the United Kingdom in Benone with spectacular views across the lough into the Republic of Ireland to Donegal. Not that Marie got to see any of it stuck behind the large concrete walls that enclosed the prison.

Marie exited through the hydraulic gates carrying a small holdall of her worldly possessions. She looked remarkably good for a woman who had been incarcerated for ten years. She was thankful Teresa had agreed to take her in until she had the chance to find a place of her own. The house she had prior to her imprisonment had long since been taken back by the council and reallocated to another family.

Marie's heart raced as she stepped out of the prison gates, feeling the sun on her skin for the first time in years. She felt like she was reborn and given a fresh start in life. She took a deep breath and closed her eyes for a moment, savouring her freedom.

As the two girls embraced, Marie felt a surge of emotions and impulsively kissed her good friend Teresa fully on the lips. She could tell it took Teresa by complete surprise. Marie, without uttering a word, reached out taking hold of Teresa's hands.

'Thank you for coming Teresa you're a true and loyal friend.' Marie almost doing a jig with her feet before saying, 'Oh come here you,' grabbing Teresa again embracing her whilst holding her extremely tight for what seemed an age. The girls had a close relationship back before Marie was imprisoned.

Investigare

They had become even closer following the death of Marie's husband. It was Teresa who stuck by her when many in the community had excluded her. They had never kissed, well at least never on the lips; it had always been on the cheeks.

Marie had a few female-on-female experiences in prison and had thought nothing of kissing her good friend. In fact, life in prison had been liberating. The two girls just stood for a moment whilst Marie took several deep breaths sucking in the intoxicating sea air which was blowing up the lough from the North Atlantic Ocean. The feeling of joy that Marie was experiencing mixed with the newfound excitement and a sense of gratitude at being released giving her the opportunity to enjoy one's independence and autonomy.

'Teresa love, I could murder a gin right now. Would the Point bar be open before we head down the road?' asked Marie.

'We could have one, but we need to get back to Belfast before the rush hour traffic as I want to take you home via the scenic route,' said Teresa.

As they walked the short distance to the bar, Marie removed her shoes. Having spent years behind bars and having been confined to a small cell with no freedom or connection to the outside world making this feel extremely liberating. As she walked barefoot, she could feel the softness of the grass beneath her feet and the grains of sand between her toes.

The gentle breeze from the Atlantic coast caressed her face, carrying with it the smell of the ocean. It was a stark contrast to the stale musty air she had grown accustomed to while incarcerated. Marie relished in the freedom of being able to breathe in the salty air and feel the coolness of the wind against her skin. She focused on the present moment, allowing the sensation of the grass and sand to ground her. Each step was a reminder of the newfound freedom she had waited so long to obtain. The grass tickled her feet with the sand providing a gentle massage as she wiggled her toes.

Reaching the bar, Marie paused to take in her surroundings. The patrons inside the bar laughed and chatted, the clinking of glasses filled the air as the ambient music played softly in the background. It was a symphony of normalcy that she had yearned for during her time in confinement.

Entering the bar, Marie felt a mix of emotions. Nervousness, excitement, and a sense of belonging all washed over her. She ordered a drink and took a seat, revelling in the simple joy of being in a crowded place, surrounded by people with lives that were not defined by prison walls.

As she sipped her drink, Marie couldn't help but smile. The journey to freedom had been gruelling, but she had made it through. And as she sat in the bar, with the feeling of the grass and sand on her feet still fresh in her memory, she knew that she would never take her newfound freedom for granted.

Having taken her time over not one but two G&T's she looked at Teresa and for the first time in an exceptionally long time, she shed a tear.

'Are you alright,' Teresa asked her concerned.

'Oh, Teresa love I'm fine, just fine, I'm happy.'

The two drinks had more of an effect than Marie had expected. She felt quite giddy and lightheaded as they got up to leave. As they made their way to the car, Marie once again removed her shoes and enjoyed the freshly mown grass beneath her feet.

The journey back to Belfast was a deliberate slow drive, taking in several of Northern Ireland's landmarks dotted along the Antrim coastal roads. They went past the old Bushmills distillery, famous for its Irish whiskey. It took all of Marie's resolve not to stop for a free sample of the world's finest brew. The Carrick-a-Rede rope bridge built in 1755 by Salmon fishermen was also visited.

Marie told Teresa, 'In all my years married to Tim, I never got to see any of these places despite them being on our doorstep.'

The girls travelled down through the villages of Ballycastle and Cushendall stopping once for a coffee in a small café overlooking the Ocean. Marie was insistent on having the window down as they travelled to allow the north Atlantic breeze to sweep through her hair.

The wind tickled her skin. She closed her eyes and took in a deep breath, feeling the cool air fill her lungs. The sound of the waves crashing against the shore was music to her ears and she couldn't help but smile. She opened her eyes and looked out at the vast expanse of water before her. The sea was a deep shade of blue, and she could see the waves crashing against the rocks as the wind continued to blow. Far off in the distance, she could see a few sailboats bobbing up and down with a backdrop of Scotland beyond.

'It's good to be free,' she said, not conscious of saying it aloud.

During the journey to Belfast the two women discussed Marie's plans and what would be her focus now that she had been released. Marie was unsure what lay ahead but had applied herself to study in prison and managed to get a degree in psychology and a diploma in law. How she intended to apply her newfound education qualifications was still unclear.

***

Teresa was still bewildered after all this time how Marie managed to carry out such a callous, calculated, and cold-blooded murder of McFarland. She had decided the human capacity for both good and evil never ceased to amaze her. *I guess hell has no fury like a woman scorned,* she thought. Teresa remembered how Marie had shouted as she was led away from court all those years back claiming she would seek retribution for all of those behind her husband's death.

Teresa had already booked tomorrow off work knowing that a visit to Sandy's bar and the downing of several glasses of wine was going to be the order of the day to celebrate Marie's release. Not that there was going to be a large reception party waiting for her, in fact many of Teresa's friends were unhappy she would even associate with the woman considering the damage inflicted on the IRA by her actions.

Teresa often had to remind them, Marie was a good friend before she went inside prison and as far as she was concerned that would not change. She would also remind them it was

Investigare

Scrappy who had Marie's husband killed and even the government had acknowledged Tim Coyle hadn't been a tout.

Chapter 6

The Funeral

The funeral for young Dermott Skelly was a very sombre and heart-breaking event. Thousands turned out for the young man from all sections of the community with church leaders from both sides of the religious divide being represented. Condemnation was swift by the leaders of all the political parties of Northern Ireland. It was a senseless loss of life of a young lad with his whole life ahead of him. It was a tragic and preventable set of circumstances.

Dermott was one of several youths taking part in a football match organised by the Black Hills shared city forum. A cross community scheme designed to remove barriers and create connections between the protestant and catholic communities from north and west Belfast.

A crowd of approximately one hundred supporters made up from parents, friends and community workers were watching an entertaining and spirited game. Bobby and Maggie Skelly, the parents of Dermott were just two of the crowd who were proudly watching their son playing. They were fully supportive of the project and hoped that closer ties with their protestant neighbours could help forge a better future for not only their own but everyone else's children. A society where they could at least live together in a more tolerant culture.

Paul "Sniffer" Horan a prominent well-known drug dealer was also at the game watching his own son play. Paul had served time for terrorist related crimes during the eighties but like so many others, was given his early release letter following the Good Friday Agreement. Paul got the nickname Sniffer because of his drug addiction and because he had no nasal septum from all the snorting he had done during his adult lifetime.

He had been warned by Declan from the New IRA that his drug dealings had been crossing boundaries and his gang of drug pushers had been encroaching not only into New IRA controlled areas but others as well and it needed to stop or he would suffer the consequences.

As Paul was watching the game, a known drug rival Bap Quinn approached and patted him on the back of his shoulders before saying, 'What bout ye Sniffer,' then moved away a few yards from him. Bap was anything but a mate of Horan.

Horan glanced to his side and seeing Bap had a questioning look on his face. The alarm bells in his head started ringing but was still going through the thought process and never noticed the heavy-set man in a balaclava, jeans, and black leather jacket walking up behind him holding a revolver pistol. Raising the gun and having had the "Collar Tap" which was the signal Bap had used for the gunman. By tapping the back of

Sniffers shoulders he therefore identified the target to the shooter.

The shooter fired three shots at the back of his head from close-range, killing Horan instantly. It all happened so quickly that Horan would have known nothing about it.

The crowd panicked as the sounds of gun fire was followed by screams that filled the air as everyone turned toward the dead man on the ground. The running shooter made his way to a waiting black Audi A3.

The getaway car exited the street at speed, but in the process narrowly missed hitting a young mother pushing a baby in its buggy across the road. The young mother fell backwards over the kerb whilst pulling the buggy close to her as she fell.

The gunman having ripped the balaclava from his head on entering the car locked eyes with the young mother as the car passed. She later give a description to the police using the confidential help line.

Back at the football pitch there was a moment of stunned silence as everyone tried to comprehend what had just occurred. The deafening and harrowing scream from Maggie Skelly brought the crowds focus back onto the playing field and the sight of the woman cradling her sons head in her lap. She couldn't believe that her precious child was gone. All the hopes and dreams she had for him were shattered in an instant. She was left with a gaping hole in her heart that she knew would never be repaired. Tears streamed down her face as she caressed his lifeless body, unable to comprehend the injustice of it all. Her mind was a jumbled mess of emotions and thoughts, as she struggled to make sense of what had happened.

Dermott's football shirt was covered in blood from the gunshot wound to his chest. His small delicate lifeless body was the latest in a long line of innocent lives to grace the killing streets of Belfast. A senseless waste of life perpetrated by the same terrorists and thugs who proclaimed to be the protectors of their communities.

They were nothing better than parasites living on the backs of the very same people they claimed to protect. Drug barons were a scourge on society. The GFA may have brought a fragile peace, but instead of terrorist related deaths from the main antagonists, it was now a country suffering a pandemic from drugs. Young Dermott Skelly becoming the latest casualty of that war.

***

The 1990's had seen a major influx of drugs into Belfast from Dublin and the UK mainland. It was particularly bad in Dublin with the introduction of weed, marijuana, followed by ecstasy which became known as the club drug. It all started with the criminals paying girls to smuggle it through the airports. The drug lords had their couriers and sellers take up positions in the most run-down inner-city apartment blocks. Some of the pushers blatantly selling from their own flats. It got so bad the Garda set up special undercover cells to target the dealers but the drug bosses were always two or three steps removed.

For a period, the residents took the law into their own hands and formed their own vigilante style groups to evict the dealers from their areas. They called themselves Concerned Parents Against Drugs (CPAD). By 1996 things were getting out of control with numerous drug related deaths as criminal gang members were being killed over territory disputes between these rival gangs all being commonplace.

Veronica Guerin a well-known investigative journalist who had tirelessly tried to get the evidence to put away the drug lords at the top of the industry was murdered by two men on a motorbike when she had stopped at traffic lights in her car on the outskirts of Dublin. It was a defining moment in the Irish Republic in its fight against drugs and its bosses. It brought about major change in the law as the newly established Asset Recovery Bureau could go after the assets of the major players and drug lords, confiscating their ill-gotten gains such as cars, property, and land. The plan was to hit the criminals where it hurt, their pockets.

***

It was common knowledge within the community that the death of Sniffer Horan was conducted under the orders of the New IRA. The fact Bap had to identify the intended target to the gunman was an indication the victim was unknown to the shooter. It was believed at the time and later confirmed by Special Branch informants that a loyalist drug lord by the name of Banter Burns and his team were responsible for the hit. It was common practice for the various factions on occasions to work together in taking out competitors.' Even Russians and Albanian gangs were starting to get in on the act.

The black Audi was found burnt out up at Silverstream in north Belfast. The city was carved up into zones controlled by the various groupings. Contract killings was just another function offered and supplied by those individuals.

Bap Quinn had approached Declan O'Hara and requested he be allowed to take out Sniffer so that they could divide up his turf, thus increasing their market share. He was happy to share the spoils but only if there was honour between thieves and no reprisals for his actions. Declan agreed to the proposal and even provided the shooter. Sniffer Horan had encroached into both Bap's and Declan's areas so he was considered a legitimate target.

These men had been senior members of the IRA with some having held positions within Sinn Fein following their release from prison. So, each of them were well known because of the profiles they held within the community. Having become disillusioned by the political process and killing being more to their taste, they decided that keeping up the pretence they were fighting for a united Ireland, but the allure of the drug money was far more lucrative and appealing.

The names of the perpetrators was known to everyone in the community. So, when Bap Quinn, Declan O'Hara, Kevin Moore, Micky Finn, Razor Fox, and Teagan Greer all turned up at the funeral of young Dermott Skelly, Maggie Skelly could not hold back her anger or contempt screaming obscenities at the six men. Her voice trembled with a mixture of anger and grief as she stared defiantly at the group of men.

'You have the blood of my dead boy on your hands.' she screamed at them. 'Get the fuck away from me, I don't want any of you scum anywhere near me or my boy.'

Bobby was stood by his wife's side, his eyes filled with tears and his fists clenched tightly. His eyes narrowed, a flicker of pain flashing across his face.

'You need to go,' Bobby Skelly said stepping across the path of his wife, making sure he used his body as a barrier worried his wife was going to attack the men.

'You're not welcome here. I want you to go and allow us the bury our child with dignity. He was just a young boy Declan. He had dreams, hopes for a future outside of this god forsaken place. You took that away from him and us. I want you to remember this moment, remember the pain you've caused us today. We hope that no other parents will have to endure what we have.'

The IRA men slowly retreated, as a sombre mood settled over the Graveyard. As Bobby held his wife tightly, their tears mingling with the earth beneath their feet, Bobby turned holding Maggie by her shoulders and said, 'They will get what's coming to them. We will have our justice. I will stop at nothing to see them all in Hell. Young Dermott Skelly was just another victim in the drug wars of Belfast.

***

Investigare

The non-descript police car parked outside the home of the Skelly family. The large Detective Sergeant (DS) Ken Stones accompanied by a female officer both being dressed in civilian clothing, locked the car, and walked up toward the front door of the house. Opening the rod iron gate, they entered the small but tidy front garden. A white two-seater bench with perfectly manicured Buxus sempervirens ball trees positioned on either side of the bench which set symmetrical under the front window.

A mobile police support car satellited the area in case of any incident that could arise from the policeman's presence at the home. The area was a republican stronghold but Ken Stones was no stranger to this part of the city having investigated numerous shooting and searches of IRA activists' houses. Not taking anything for granted, he was armed with a SIG Sauer 229 pistol tucked into his waistband and a further small ankle holster SIG Sauer 230.

There was something quite different about this house and the people who lived in it. It didn't have the same Maze prison produced souvenirs associated with republicanism. What struck Ken as he entered the house was the picture in the hall of a soldier in an Ulster Rifles uniform. The small plaque on the bottom of the picture read, Corporal Skelly, "Happy Valley," Korea 1951.

A neighbour and friend of the family showed Ken into the lounge where Bobby and Maggie were seated. The neighbour not asking who he was but rather assuming he was there to pay his respects and offer his condolences as many members of the community had been doing since the death of young Dermott.

Bobby was sitting next to his wife with his arm around her shoulder comforting her. A tired looking Bobby looked up as Ken Stones entered the room but Maggie remained with her head bowed rotating a set of rosary beads between thumb and forefinger.

'Mr Skelly, My name is Detective Sergeant Ken Stones and I'm so very sorry for your loss. I apologise for this intrusion at this time but it's important I ask you a few questions concerning the events of last week and the tragic circumstances that occurred.'

'Can you not see we're grieving here and my wife is in no fit state to discuss anything. She has had to be sedated, filled with pills, and can barely talk. We have just buried our son for goodness' sake,' said Bobby.

'I completely understand, believe me I do, I have been where you are right now and I know how difficult this is for you.

'How the hell do you understand what I'm going through. You might go to the homes of victims and express your sympathy in the line of duty, but I have lost my boy. You couldn't possibly know what we're going through,' stated Bobby.

Ken explained, 'I too have lost a son to the barbaric scum such as those who set up and fired the fatal shots that killed your boy. My own son was killed whilst playing in his bedroom. A place he should have been secure and safe, The terrorists conducted a drive by shooting, spraying the front of the house with bullets. My lad was near the window when the sporadic shooting started and he was hit and killed. So, Bobby, I know exactly how you're feeling, and my heart goes out to you.'

Bobby listened and even Maggie became responsive to what was being said. There was an acceptance by Bobby that the conversation between Detective Ken Stones and himself was filled with genuine compassion and understanding. Stones expressed his heartfelt condolences, acknowledging the immense pain and sorrow that Skelly must be experiencing after losing his son.

This tragedy had deeply affected Stones and had given him a unique perspective on the immense grief that Skelly was currently enduring. Knowing the depth of his own sorrow and the challenges he had faced while dealing with his own loss, Detective Stones made it a point to offer Skelly any support and guidance he could provide. He understood the long and painful journey ahead for Skelly, and he wanted to ensure that the grieving father felt supported and understood during this grim time.

He became not only a detective investigating a tragic crime, but also a source of comfort and understanding for someone who was facing the unimaginable pain of losing a child. However, this did not diminish Bobby Skelly's hatred for the perpetrators with him reminding DS Stones his desire to get justice and openly stated, 'I will seek retribution myself if the police don't bring these scumbags before the courts.'

'Bobby, I can't stress this enough, Maggie needs you and doing anything stupid will only add to her stress. Family is so important. Both of you are grieving. I promise you and Maggie,

I will do everything in my power to hunt down those responsible.'

He was offered tea and accepted as he talked to Bobby whilst showing empathy for their situation. '

I couldn't help but notice the picture in your hallway as I came in, said DS Stones. I assume it's your father going on the likeness.

'Yes, he was a proud man who had served several years in the Ulster Rifles. The picture was taken when he was in Korea. He didn't talk much about his time there, only stating he had seen some unforgettable sights. My only regret was I never got to follow in his footsteps. I guess the pressures of living were we did and the outbreak of the "Troubles" made it impossible to enlist back then. When he was discharged, he bought out my grandfather from his butcher business which I now have stewardship.'

The two men chatted for some considerable time with DS stones able to craft his art of interviewing whilst still managing to gain what he needed without being over formal.

DS Stone had a reputation for being an exceptional interviewer. He had a unique skill of extracting the information he needed without making his subjects feel interrogated or overwhelmed by formality. His approach was effortless, yet effective.

As they continued to chat, DS Stone adeptly steered the conversation towards the topics he wanted to explore. He carefully chose his words and asked open-ended questions that encouraged Bobby Skelly to share his thoughts freely. He listened intently, genuinely interested in what the man had to say. Bringing the interview to a close, he stood to excuse himself when Maggie spoke for the first time looking directly at DS Stones declaring, 'O'Hara is responsible, him and his cronies.'

Ken Stones, responded, speaking directly to Maggie he stated.

'I will get them, trust me.'

It was Bobby who had the last words saying. 'If you don't I will.'

Chapter 7

The Meeting

Following the funeral of young Dermott Skelly, a meeting between Bap and his team of pushers took place at a safe house in the Lenadoon area of Belfast. Four men were seated around the kitchen table with Bap taking a standing position with his back to the kitchen sink with the window and its filthy yard behind him. The owner of the house had made herself scarce by retiring upstairs with her fix of heroin. This being her reward for the use of the house for the meetings. Her dependency on the drug making it an easy business arrangement between the parties.

Bap started by ripping into those present over poor drug sales from their respective pitches.

'Listen you lot, sales are down and some of you aren't pulling your weight. There better be an improvement otherwise someone will suffer. Do I make myself clear?'

'That bastard Sniffer Horan tried to muscle in on our area and you know what happened to him. At least two local businesses have had demands for protection money on a few separate occasions last month and it had been Horan's men.' Bap knew he couldn't have dealt with it on his own for fear of an all-out turf war, at least not without help from others. He explained, 'I dealt with that matter.' Although he was stating the obvious as nothing but the Horan murder and the kid's death was all that was being discussed about town.

The funeral for Horan was a much smaller affair than that of young Skelly. A small congregation consisting of the immediate family and a brazen few of his team of drug pushers. Other close associates opting to avoid attending for fear they may have been on the hit list. However, what was evident, was the fact they had lost control of their share of the market.

Bap turned his attention to Gerry Finnegan, whose drug sales were by far the worst of the team. Looking directly at Gerry he stated, 'Your money is way down and regardless of excuse's; money needs to be returned for the drugs you claim have yet to dispose of.'

Gerry tried to justify his short comings by stating,

'I'm still owed money and will have it soon, I promise.'

Bap knew exactly the reason for the shortfall but was hoping Gerry would come clean and admit he had been dipping into the takings. Although married, Bap knew Gerry had been frequenting several of the massage parlours in the area and therefore the issue of money being syphoned off the top was Bap's main concern. Bap had not decided what course of action he should take with Gerry but he had a short fuse and even by his standards could not have envisaged his next move. Acting on impulse and a fit of anger he walked to the rear of Gerry and removing a 9mm pistol from his waistband shot Gerry in the back of the head. The two men at either end of the table bounced back out of their chairs away from the table landing on their backs on the floor, but Jerome who had been sitting directly opposite Gerry was set frozen in his seat in a state of shock, covered in blood and brain matter. The body of Gerry was face down on the table with an ever-increasing crimson pool of blood forming around his head which was slowly cascading across the table. Eventually Jerome found his voice and shouted, 'What the fuck Bap.'

'The bastard has been holding out on me and got what he deserves,' said Bap. He then continued by stating,

'If any of you fuckers think you can get one over on me, then think again, because I'll not hesitate to "Nutt" you as well.' Looking down at the body still slumped in his chair he said, 'Had the fucker never heard of Bromide.' Then give a sadistic chuckle.

There was a loud thud followed by a series of bangs coming from the direction of the hall. On opening the kitchen door, they found Shona, the lady of the house lying in a heap at the bottom of the stairs. *She must have heard the gun shot and stumbled towards the landing, tripping, and tumbling all the way down the stairs*, Thought Bap. Although still conscious but incoherent, she still had a large rubber band tied around her upper arm. Shona was carried back up the stairs and thrown on top of the bed in the rear bedroom and left to live out her intoxicating hallucinations from her recent fix.

Investigare

The disposal of Gerry Finnegan's body became the team's priority. Gerry was dumped in an alleyway with a small quantity of drugs spattered around the body and the pockets of his jacket ripped to give the appearance of a drug robbery having taken place. It was hoped that it would go down as a "Tit for Tat" attack following Horan's murder.

Chapter 8

The Stranger

The night was cold and the sky shrouded in cloud making it darker than normal for the time of night. The man was not expecting the bitterly chilly wind as he left his home on his way to Sandy's bar. He pulled tight on his coat trying hard to shield himself against the bitterly biting breeze that was present. As he walked along the quiet street, he could see through the windows of his neighbours' houses and had second thoughts about going out seeing how cosy and inviting they appeared.

Another bloody meeting, he thought. *What could be so bloody important it couldn't wait until tomorrow.*

The call had come just before six that evening. He didn't recognise the caller but then he had been asleep on his settee at the time the call came through and wasn't concentrated. He was startled when the telephone rang. The caller was brief but clear by stating, 'The foreigner will be in Sandy's 8:30pm.' The recognised codeword "Foreigner" was given, so he had no reason to doubt the authenticity of the call or caller.

Investigare

The funnel of warm air being expelled from his mouth clearly demonstrating just how cold the night was. He cupped his hands in front of his face trying desperately to heat them. He never noticed the figure lurking on the far side of the street in the shadows next to the alleyway. He continued walking toward the end of the street. As he passed the lamp post his shadow was cast onto the gable wall exaggerating and distorting his body, making him appear hunched and disfigured.

Thinking he heard footsteps behind him, he looked back over his left shoulder in the direction of his house but detected nothing untoward. The street appeared empty with only the sound of his own breath and footsteps penetrating the night air. He turned back pulling up his collar and placing his hands deep into his pockets for warmth.

The street had always been his home. Despite many in Sinn Fein and the IRA opting for holiday homes in Donegal or moving to larger houses in the more affluent areas of the city. This all made possible on the proceeds of the extortion and drug peddling over the years. Many in the community believing the proceeds of the Northern bank robbery helped in their procurement of the holiday homes.

He had always been comfortable with his lot, although he did splash out now and again on expensive and lavish holidays abroad. He believed he had earned his reward; He had served his time at her majesty's pleasure and had been a resolute and seasoned volunteer of the IRA.

Having been instrumental in the Maze breakout in the eighties and having been the head of communications for Sinn Fein following his release, he had become disillusioned in Sinn

Fein's line of diplomacy. He was a republican and activist who wanted to continue with the arms struggle against the British State. He had been an active service member for over twenty years but believed it was a young man's game now. He didn't need to get his hands dirty but was still an executive officer for the New IRA which he and a few hard-line ex PIRA members gravitated too following the GFA.

***

Having placed the telephone call there was still time to kill before going to the Springfield Road and the home of the intended target. Observing the target was easy due to the early winter nights and the target showing a distinct lack of awareness with the curtains to the lounge not being closed. The internal lights were exposing the occupant of the property. The target was watched as he prepared to leave the house.

The stranger thought, *what poor security awareness by the target and him being such a high-profile republican activist.*

When sure the target was about to leave the house, the stranger retreated across the street taking up a position within the alleyway, being appreciative for the poor lighting which helped with concealment. The stranger watched as the target made his way along the street before stepping out of the alleyway and maintaining a discrete distance so as not to be compromised.

Investigare

At one point the target stopped and turned looking over his shoulder but the stranger managed to crouch down behind a parked car to avoid being detected. *Had the target glanced over his right shoulder instead of his left, he may have caught a glimpse of the stranger.* Thought the Stranger.

For two weeks the stranger had been watching the target as he went about the city with numerous visits to several houses of known criminals. The Stranger had observed these properties and the frequent comings and goings of the visitors.

From the observations it was clear these properties were being used for the supply of drugs. All of this was taking place a few hundred yards from the offices of Sinn Fein. The names of Gary McSweeney and Jean Devlin were printed on either side of the large Sinn Fein sign with its green map of Ireland and its gold and white letters of SF symbolised across it. The café across the street from one of the houses had provided excellent cover enabling the stranger to observe the target.

During the period of surveillance, the target had visited Sandy's bar on four separate occasions and each time had taken the same route to and from the bar. The republican bar had been renamed after Bobby Sands who had died during the hunger strikes of the eighties at the Maze prison, which republicans called "Long Kesh." It was hoped tonight would be no different for the strangers long-awaited plan to work.

The target reached the end of the street and turned left crossing the road using waste ground as a short cut. The place used to be a small shirt factory long since closed. It consisted of two buildings with a small pathway between them. It used to provide much needed employment to the area.

The pathway led to a six-foot perimeter fence which was also in a state of disrepair and gapped enabling passage through it. As the target turned into the gap, he became aware that someone was directly behind him. He turned quickly and came face to face with the stranger. He was within inches of the stranger that he could feel the warm air being expelled from the out of breath stranger's mouth.

***

The stranger seeing the target reach the street corner had to increase the pace for fear of losing the element of surprise or opportunity, having designated the old shirt factory as the area to affect the plan. Running across the road and entering the small carpark of the old shirt factory, the stranger observed the target go between the buildings. The stranger thought, *it's now or never* and ran into the gap only to collide with the target who had heard the approaching footsteps and turned to see who or what was closing in on him.

There was a momentary face to face and eye contact as the bodies collided with each other. For an instant, the target attempted to recall where he had seen this person before but continued to struggle to recall a time or place.

The rapid intake of breath was toiled with the feeling and sensation something was very wrong. He had the feeling of warm liquid running down his stomach seeping into the waistband of his trousers. His breathing became profoundly laboured with each breath becoming shorter and shorter. His body became weak as he looked down at the knife embedded just below his breastbone.

The look of confusion was now spread across his face as he realised the severity of his injury. He stumbled forward before eventually unable to remain upright slid down onto his knees. He was now feeling weak and dizzy. Panic set in as he struggled to stay conscious, knowing that his only chance of survival was to get away but he had no energy to flee or fight. Looking up at the stranger he was still trying to make sense of what had just occurred.

The stranger was determined not to allow the target to simply bleed out but wanted it to be a callous, vicious, and a merciless murder. The knife was removed and with a thrust of the strangers' right hand, it was forced into the throat of the target. The stranger stepping back to avoid the blood surges now gushing from the throat wound as the target fell flat on the ground. With his eyes still wide open and staring at the feet of the stranger he gasped for his last breaths. The voice of the stranger who was now crouched beside him said, 'Rot in hell Teagan Greer,' before stepping over the body and disappearing into the cold damp night.

***

A dog walker found the body of Teagan Greer early in the morning. It was a gruesome discovery. Greer had been stabbed in the chest and had his throat cut. The dog walker thought, *whoever committed the dastardly act had showed no mercy.* It was reported by the news outlets as overkill.

The news was received by Declan O'Hara with complete shock and disgust. It was a catastrophic loss for them. There were no leads as to who or why he had been butchered. Of course, he would have had many enemies, some within his own community but Loyalists would also have him on their target list, particularly the drug fraternity. The only certainty was the Security Services wouldn't be losing any sleep over his demise.

***

The Criminal Investigation Department (CID) and their Crime Scene Investigation (CSI) found nothing at the crime scene in way of evidence to identify the culprit. Despite a thorough search of the area for evidence, no weapon, DNA samples, fingerprints, or other materials that may have been connected to the crime was found. They meticulously checked the area half expecting that there would have been a struggle leaving some sort of evidence. They also looked for any physical evidence present, such as fibres or hairs, but again nothing of note was found that could be sent to the laboratory for analysis.

The team believed the perpetrator must have worn gloves but even if they had worn latex the high-tech equipment available to forensics surely would have picked up something. But that wasn't the case.

Investigare

There was a great deal of interest by the press who had converged to the scene once the news had broken. Police cameras scanned the area and all those present in case the perpetrator had returned to the scene of the crime to watch proceedings unfold.

Micky Finn was one of many observers who watched as the forensic team worked as the police managed the cordon now in place. Speculation was ripe with Loyalist paramilitaries being the prime suspects.

The leading police investigator, Detective Sergeant Ken Stones was quick to speculate that it was drugs related.

'One way or another this is drug related said DS Stones,' I would bet my house on it, 'he concluded.

Of course, denial was swift from all the factions including INLA. They were worried the finger of suspicion would be pointed at them, because of their refusal to toe the line following several altercations between the two terrorist organisations in recent times. The power struggle for the lucrative drugs trade and area dominance being deemed reason enough.

Several associates and team members arrived at Declan's to try and determine who may have been responsible. Micky Finn was quick to blame rival drug gangs for the murder. A little too quick in Declan's opinion.

Declan was always uneasy about Micky who had delusions of grandeur. Razor had warned Declan on numerous occasions by saying, 'Keep your friends close but your enemy's closer' when referring to Micky as he has dangerous ambitions and frig whoever got in his way.' Declan was conscious of it and always kept Micky at arm's length but was acutely aware he needed to watch his back.

***

The knock at the door woke both girls up out of their sleep. Still drowsy and dressed in her dressing gown, Teresa went down the stairs shouting at whoever was on the other side of the door responsible for the banging to pack it in, shouting, 'Alright …alright, hold on I'm bloody coming.'

On opening the door, she was shocked to see police officers standing on her doorstep.

'Sorry for the intrusion,' said the female officer accompanied by her male colleague. 'I would like to speak with Marie Coyle.'

'What for?' demanded Teresa.

'Is she in?' enquired the officer.

'Who is it?' shouted Marie from the top of the stairs.

'It's the bloody police looking for you, responded Teresa.

'What the hell,' Marie said as she made her way down the stairs to be greeted by the two police officers and her shocked house mate.

'What's going on Marie?' asked Teresa.

'How to hell should I know,' responded Marie before turning to the police officer and asking the same question,

'What's going on?'

'We need to ask you a few questions about your movements last night, but it would be better if you accompanied us down to the station.'

'I'm going nowhere until you tell me what this is all about, said an adamant Marie.'

'Listen lets not make this any more difficult than it needs to be' piped in the male officer conscious they didn't want to be hanging around in the area any longer than necessary. Both officers being fearful their presence in the area could spark a lot of hostility.

'We just want to eliminate you from our enquiries that's all,' said the female officer.

'I have been here all night with Teresa stated Marie.'

Teresa having retrieved her phone was next to speak looking directly at Marie and said, 'Holy shit, Teagan Greer was murdered last night and its all-over social media.' Teresa looked again concerningly at Marie but there was no obvious reaction. Teresa had a horrible feeling that her good friend had been in some way involved but said nothing. Teresa's mind raced as she tried to process the shocking news. Teagan Greer had been one of Scrappy's boys back in the day and a member of the New IRA.

She glanced back at Marie, searching for any sign of guilt or involvement, but found none.

Teresa's gut instinct whispered that Marie knew more than she let on. Despite having been friends for years and having shared secrets and supporting each other through thick and thin but right now, in the face of such devastating news, Teresa couldn't help but question if she truly knew Marie at all. She had been convinced Marie had paid her debt to society and was seeking a better life free from her baggage of the past.

The female officer reiterated, 'We just want to eliminate you from our enquiries.'

Marie got dressed and accompanied the two officers to the station. She had spent several hours at the station before being released and returning home. Not having any evidence and accepting what had been said on the doorstep that both girls had spent the evening together, she was told she was free to go.

***

Teresa had spent the hours Marie was away dissecting everything from that morning. The fact she lied to the police by giving Marie the alibi made her extremely uncomfortable. She had not been with Marie all evening. Marie had been out God knows where. She needed to speak with Marie but wasn't looking forward to it. Once Marie had returned Teresa wasted no time in addressing the elephant in the room.

'Marie,' her voice trembling. 'Do you... do you know anything about this, Marie?'

Marie's face remained impassive, but her eyes flickered with something Teresa couldn't quite decipher.

'I... I don't know anything Teresa,' she finally replied. Her voice wavered slightly, revealing hints of underlying emotions.

Teresa desperately wanted to believe Marie, to hold onto their friendship and trust. But doubt lingered, poisoning the memories they had shared. Swallowing her apprehension, a nervous Teresa said, 'Marie, then why did I have to lie about you being here with me?'

'If I had said I was out last night they would have held me much longer and tried to put the blame on me, that's why. I didn't do it Teresa.'

Teresa couldn't help but feel that her relationship with Marie once filled with laughter and companionship, was spiralling into a dark and treacherous unknown.

Chapter 9

Birthday Treat

Sean decided to treat his son Peter for his 21st birthday by taking him to Manchester for a testimonial friendly football match between Manchester United and Celtic. Sean had always supported Manchester United with Peter being a big Celtic supporter, well at least from afar.

Despite Glasgow only a short train journey from Dumfries the family decided the city was to be permanently off limits to them. Sean felt the journey down to Manchester wouldn't cause them any concerns as most Celtic supporters from back home mainly stuck to going to the Glasgow matches.

As part of his treat, Sean booked a tour of the stadium which was more for his own guilty pleasure than Peter's. They both travelled down and having arrived at Piccadilly Station, got a taxi straight to Old Trafford.

Both men enjoyed the guided tour getting to see the trophy cabinet, dressing rooms, and even getting onto the pitch. Peter looked at all the old pictures of Irish players who had played over the years for United and revelled in the names such as

George Best, Harry Gregg who was the goalkeeper and one of the Busby Babes. Other names such as Norman Whiteside, Denis Irwin and Sammy McIlroy and even less well-known name from home, George Spiers.

On leaving the hall of fame and trophy room, they were taken onto the pitch. Stepping onto the perfectly manicured grass, they couldn't help but imagine the roar of the crowd reverberating through the stands. It was a truly breathtaking sight, with the stadium's steep seats seemingly reaching for the sky, enveloping the pitch in an embrace.

Standing in the centre, Sean took in every detail. The sense of history of battles fought and victories won, was overwhelming. he thought again about the countless players displayed on the walls who had graced this field and the moments of pure magic that had unfolded before the eyes of millions of fans.

It was a memorable trip with both men being satisfied with the match result being a hard fought 2-2 draw.

Following the game, the men made their way back to Manchester Piccadilly station for the journey home. Onboard the train and halfway through the three-hour trip to Carlisle, Sean asked Peter if he wanted anything from the buffet carriage before leaving him to go and fetch two hot drinks.

As Sean exited the carriage a tall overweight man with a large scar down his right cheek and short greying hair leant out of his seat and watched Sean exit the carriage, this being observed by Peter. On Sean's return, Peter leant over to his dad and whispered, 'Don't look now but a man about six seats down on the left watched you leave and return to the carriage, but wasn't just watching, I think he recognises you.'

'Christ son… that's not good. Are you sure he was looking at me?'

'Definitely, it was like he was trying hard to remember how he knew you,' said Peter.

'What does he look like,' asked Sean without looking back.

'He looks tall and fat with grey hair and has a large scar on his right cheek.'

'What do you mean by a scar?'

'A big scar from his ear to his lip.'

It was evident Sean was worried as he became subdued. The remainder of the trip was nerve racking for the pair who were rooted to their seats not daring to move. The man did not approach them, much to Sean's relief. Peter noticed his Dad's demeanour had changed as he appeared to be deep in thought which was only interrupted by the trains tannoy as it announced the trains arrival at Carlisle station informing passengers they should change at Carlisle for "Dumfries, Hexham and Kilmarnock."

As soon as the train stopped both men waited until the last possible moment before rushing out of the carriage in the opposite direction to where the man was seated and onto the platform. The train started moving again and as their carriage passed them, the man Peter had described was staring directly at Sean drawing his index finger of his right hand across his throat in a left to right motion. Sean took a deep intake of breath, his suspicions confirmed and said, 'Fucking hell it's Razor Fox.'

Chapter 10

The Hunt

The visit by Razor Fox to the home of Declan was very much welcomed. Razor started by saying, 'I'm sure I recognised Steven Tierney on the train to Glasgow and the look on his face told me that Tierney recognised me. He was along with a lad probably in his twenties and the spit of Steven. So, I would guess it's his son.'

Declan, rubbing his hands together triumphantly said, 'fucking five years I've waited to find that bastard and the wee shite has been in Glasgow the whole friggin time.'

'I never said that. He got off the train in Carlisle and I don't know if he did because he lived there or because he was trying to avoid me, it was the first stop he could have got off, said Razor.

'Christ that doesn't help me, does it?' said Declan.

Razor stated, 'passengers change for three other destinations at Carlisle such as Dumfries, Hexham, and even

Kilmarnock so he could be going to any of them, or he could simply live in Carlisle.'

'Well then, that narrows it down,' Declan said sarcastically. 'Frig he could be living in Glasgow for all we know.'

'Declan, I don't believe he's in Glasgow as there are too many republicans aligned to us for him to be there, but he didn't have any luggage, only a small duffle bag so I would say they were definitely heading home,' said Razor.

'Right then, I will reach out to our good friend Jock McClean in Glasgow and get him and his team to put the feelers out. I'm also happy to fund a team to go around the other places if needed to flush him out,' said Declan.

***

Jock McClean was the head of the Glasgow operation. A long-distance lorry driver by profession, but a convicted republican activist who had served several jail terms for drug trafficking and extortion over the years.

***

The trip back to Heathhall was very subdued with very little chat between the two men. Peter did ask his Dad, 'Are we going to have to move because of this?'

'No… Razor saw us in Carlisle so we don't have to worry.' But Sean was worried. The following weeks were far from ideal, every car and pedestrian that passed the home cottage were spied upon from behind the curtains.

The daily trips into Dumfries to the bookshop were cautious affairs. Extra vigilance was used with Sean even changing the routing into Dumfries by using the ring road and entering the town from alternate directions. It took him back to when he first came to the area. The feeling of paranoia he demonstrated, worrying that he was being followed or watched. It took almost the first year for his anxiety to wane. But following his encounter with Razor Fox he was right back where he had started.

Just as he started to feel a bit less anxious, he was visited by Sammy Carson his old handler. Sammy hadn't seen Sean in several years having left the force and taken up classified intelligence contractual work in various world hot spots including IRAQ and Afghanistan. He also had his own surveillance company in Northern Ireland which he partnered with a few close associates Roy and Davy from his time in the forces.

He was accompanied by Kathy a member of MI5 and who had been assigned the Talbot case since their arrival on the mainland. Kathy took the lead and spoke first to Sean by stating,

'Information has come to light that activists from Glasgow have been making enquiries concerning your whereabouts. A well-placed Agent within the republican criminal network in Glasgow reported you were last seen in Carlisle four weeks ago.'

Sean conveyed his side of the story concerning his encounter with Razor Fox.

What Sammy and Kathy never divulged to the Talbot family was the concern they had following the interception of telephone calls between Declan O'Hara and Jock McClean. Telephone security was taken very seriously by the IRA but despite taking what they believed was good security precautions their phones were still continuously being monitored. Unfortunately, there was now a real threat of a team or individuals from Belfast coming over to search for the family and in particular Sean. If the other members of the family got in the way, then they would simply be classed as collateral damage.

There was no talk of moving the family yet but an increase in vigilance was suggested or more to the point, recommended. Special Branch and MI5 were monitoring any known republican activists entering the country with extra checks on all the seaports and airports.

***

The Glasgow cell had travelled to Carlisle but had found nothing of interest. Bars and nightclubs had been visited not so much looking for Sean but the younger Peter in the hope he would lead them to his dad. In addition, Declan had tasked a librarian by the name of Teresa Stitt to search the internet for

Investigare

any news reports from the local newspapers connected with any of the reported locations.

He asked her to concentrate on the period 1996-1997 but also look at colleges in the areas for intakes and photos of students. This was the timeframe he believed the Tierney family would have been relocated to the mainland. Teresa wasn't keen to do the task but decided she would go along with it to avoid any adverse comeback.

It was a pain staking task with nothing to go on. Teresa did find a small article in the Dumfries echo which fitted the period given. She had initially glanced over it as she had been straining for hours on the computer. The name Talbot caught her eye having mistakenly read it. *A case of phonological deficit*, She thought, but for some reason it made her go back to the small piece which read:

The chamber of commerce for the Dumfries and Galloway district would like to welcome Mr Sean Talbot and his family to the business community and wish them every success in the recently established "The Reading Room" bookshop.

Not believing it would lead anywhere the information was passed to Declan and following his own analytical assessment, concluded that it fitted in with the requested period and the area matched the train routing from Carlisle. Of course, he would have expected the Tierney family to be given completely new identities by the Security Service. Maybe the initials of S T was just a coincidence but one which he could determine easily enough. A quick search on the internet found the shop and the telephone number.

Jock McClean was tasked with making the call so as not to spook whoever answered. A Scottish caller wouldn't raise the same suspicions as an Irish caller. A simple enquiry requesting the shops opening hours was decided upon. This would at least identify if the owner was Irish.

The call was placed and much to Declan's delight, it was answered by an Irish accented male. Further clarity was needed to the identity of the bookshop owner. So, it was decided the send someone from Glasgow to Dumfries to obtain photographic evidence of the owner.

Jock had the appearance of a thug and someone who couldn't spell book never mind read one. Therefore, he was immediately ruled out but he would send a trusted female as replacement for himself in Morag McConnachie.

Morag was a slim build darkhaired single woman in her thirties. She worked as a medical sales representative and travelled the length and breadth of the country selling her medicines, prescription drugs and medical equipment to GP's and pharmacies. It had been an excellent cover enabling her to supply drugs to the republican group. She had acted as a courier for several years with a perfect cover. Morag had been recruited whilst at university in Edinburgh when she was still studying for her degree in medicine.

***

The Silver Birch hotel in Dumfries was chosen for one night and booked under her own name. It was considered a low-risk

Investigare

operation with one simple task. She was expected to visit the bookshop shortly after it opened and obtain a photograph of the owner which would be forwarded immediately to Jock for processing and dissemination back to Belfast.

On her arrival in Dumfries, Morag went into the town centre to locate "The Reading Room" bookshop. Once she was happy of its location and route to it, she went and booked into the hotel. Having settled into her room she went down to the hotel restaurant for her evening meal. This was routine for Morag as she would often be required to stay over during her travels in the course of her work. She already had another appointment booked at a pharmacy in Carlisle following her little task in Dumfries.

All in a day's work, she thought.

The restaurant was small but quaint and quiet. She thought to herself that the tables were a little too close together which give a certain feeling of being closed in. This wasn't helped when a gentleman took a seat at the next table to Morag. Although the tables were separated and both individuals were seated at the opposite ends of their respective tables, they were still very much in each other's eyeline. Morag Thought, *an empty beach and then someone comes and sits right next to you.* That was the feeling she had. If she had reached out a hand, she would have been able to touch the man.

'Good evening. Are you here on business or pleasure?' asked the man.

Taken by surprise she said, 'No…yes, I'm sorry, I'm just passing through, I have an appointment in Carlisle tomorrow.'

'Oh, right, I'm sorry, I didn't mean to pry, it's just that with it being Robbie Burns week, I thought you might be here for one of the many "Robert Burns" readings and gatherings.'

Morag hadn't considered the Burns events or the fact many bookshops might be extremely busy. A small oversight in the timing of the visit but an oversight, nonetheless.

It should however provide me with additional cover when I enter, she thought.

'Hi, I'm Josh,' the man said reaching out a hand to shake. Morag responded by extending her hand and introducing herself.

'Slainte Mhath,' Josh said.

'I beg your pardon,' Morag responded!'

John laughed and said, 'it means, Happy Burns Night.'

'Oh, I see,' said Morag, 'but what you said is actually pronounced, Slanj-uhva,' and it means "Good Health" and laughed.

'Well, I beg your pardon, you clearly know your Burns.'

'No, just Gaelic. But you could have said, "Oidhche Bhlas Burns" which really is…Happy Burns Night.'

Josh held his hands in the air demonstrating his surrender, deciding to quit rather than dig an even bigger hole with his poor Gaelic knowledge. Josh managed to keep the conversation going throughout dinner, well at least long enough for his female colleague Gabby from MI5 to finish searching Morag's room and placing a tracker on her car.

Chapter 11

Doctors Orders

Sammy and Kathy arrived at the home of the Talbot family. Kathy had informed Sean that a further member of the team would arrive later that evening and would be there to assist in the coming days. He would remain in the house as additional protection.

This was a scenario Sean had dreaded but a consequence of his own actions and what he described himself as, "hiding in plain sight." He now knew that Declan O'Hara was hunting him and conceded that he would never give up until he got his man. For a split second he had a terrible thought of striking first. *Could I take Declan out, could I go back to Belfast and end this torment. Maybe I could come clean and seek forgiveness.*

You're being an idiot, he told himself and put the thought out of his head. This was his new life now, whatever that meant.

The family were seated in the lounge then Kathy explained,

'We have identified a female who is already in the local area having travelled down from Glasgow to Dumfries in a bid to establish your identity. The analyst at MI5's Communications Centre had been a busy boy with the telephone exchanges between O'Hara and someone in Glasgow.'

'Who in Glasgow?' Steven asked.

'That's not important and you don't need to know,' Sammy added. 'All you need to know is that we're here to make sure you and your family aren't compromised.'

'We have a plan of action which we will go through when the other member of the team arrives later,' said Kathy.

Steven had a million questions but knew he wouldn't get the answers he was seeking from Kathy or Sammy, but he trusted them impeccably.

Just after 10pm a knock came at the front door and following a radio call from the surveillance team, Kathy let the third member of the team into the house. After the introductions and a good old cup of tea, the Talbot's were briefed on the plan for the following morning.

The intelligence report which had been corroborated by other intelligence assets reporting in Glasgow stated,

The "Doctor" was going to Dumfries to conduct a medical review. It was confirmed the doctor was a female medical salesperson known to MI5 as Morag McConnachie.

A surveillance team from MI5's, "4A" had followed Morag for the duration of the journey from Glasgow to Dumfries. A second team from MI5, Josh and Gabby had already been at the Silver Birch hotel when Morag arrived. The plan was set.

Chapter 11

Deception

Poetry in Motion

Subterfuge was the order of the day. Morag had breakfast at the hotel watched by Josh. Gabby remained out of sight. Polite conversation was had between both parties with Morag stating she would be going to Carlisle later in the morning. Josh stated he would be going north to Edinburgh on business. Having had breakfast, they returned to their respective rooms to prepare for checkout.

Morag was in the process of putting the remainder of her overnight clothing into her bag when she suddenly stopped and looked down at the PV900 covert camera which Jock had given her. It was where she had left it in the bedside drawer but she was sure it was facing the wrong way. She tried to recall how she had put the phone like device into the drawer.

Morag was sure she had placed it face up so as not to damage the screen, yet it was now face down. She struggled to remember if she had moved it again on her return from dinner the previous evening. Having only consumed two small glasses of wine with her dinner she was sure she wasn't mistaken. She stood pondering and looking around the room for anything that seemed out of place or disturbed but eventually dismissed the thought, placing the device in her bag.

***

The video footage recovered from the device the previous evening by Gabby showed Jock demonstrating how the device should be used. It was similar in size to a small phone and even had the appearance of one. It could be set down flat on a table or simply held in your hand and could be used to either record or take photo stills of her intended target. An excellent covert device but Jock had failed to clean it down prior to giving it to Morag.

***

Breakfast in the Talbot household was provided by Rita, Sean's wife and it was the first decent fry up Sammy had since his call for assistance back from Afghanistan. The telephone call had

Investigare

come just at the right time. His contract as a special advisor to the Afghanistan National Army Special Operations Command (ANASOC), had just ended. He had been sitting on the airfield at Hamid Karzai International Airport in Kabul when he got the call. He had a soft spot for Sean as they had an exceptionally good working relationship over the ten odd years in province. The relocation of the Tierney family to the mainland weighed heavy on his conscience so the call for assistance was answered enthusiastically by Sammy.

***

Morag was triggered away from the hotel by the surveillance team and loosely followed to the town centre of Dumfries. The tracker was working fine so the team didn't need to get too close and were able to satellite along parallel roads even managing to get ahead of the target to trigger her through various choke points. Josh and Gabby waited until Morag was clear from the hotel before calling an end to their part in the operation.

***

The Range Rover belonging to the Talbot's left the house as normal and made its way to "The Reading Room" bookshop. The shop was opened on time and within minutes of the shutters going up, the first customers were going through the doors. It was a large shop but it was a bit of a labyrinth. Shelves seemed to twist and turn in various directions. One large, angled mirror above the counter being the main surveillance apparatus for the customers perusing the shelves of books.

Two large bay windows with small Georgian style frames were located on either side of the main door. Some of the small windows acted like picture frames displaying books to the outside world. The bays of the windows housed benches and stools for the customers convenience.

A small coin operated hot drinks machine provided the only refreshments on offer. A small child's table with four school style Victorian wooden chairs being the only other available seating. These were situated in the centre of the shop front. This was used by children as parents browsed the shelves for their own reading pleasures.

***

Morag parked her car at one of the public carparks adjacent to the river Nith. She then walked the short distance back into the centre where she was triggered into the shop by the surveillance team. On entering the shop, Morag made her way to the many aisles of books on display. She was greeted by the man behind the counter who introduced himself as Sean and stated, 'If there is anything you need don't hesitate to ask.'

Investigare

'I'm fine at the moment, I'm just browsing thanks,' Morag responded.

'OK love, just shout if you need me,' was the response in a strong Irish accent accompanied with a confident and flirtatious smile. Morag smiled at the man and continued browsing. After several minutes she returned from the Labyrinth of shelves and took a seat in the window. She placed her PV900 on the bench with its lens pointing back toward the counter and started recording.

Everything she had been told about this man didn't fit. For one, he looked at least ten years older than the described Steven Tierney. He was also taller and broader than expected. As she was mentally logging the details of her target, a female entered the shop and went straight over to the man and kissed him full on his lips before saying in an English accent, 'You left before I had a chance to say goodbye this morning, I'm just going into town to get a few things and then I'll see you back here for lunch love.'

'Go easy on the card,' he said with a laugh.

The Lady left the shop waving the back of her hand in a facetious manor without turning back toward the man.

Morag was satisfied she had sufficient footage of the man and his wife or partner. She took the small book of poems she had been looking at to the counter and paid for it before thanking the man. Being satisfied with her task and believing she had achieved her mission; she exited the shop.

***

The post operation wash up or debrief was conducted back at the Talbot family home. Sammy emerged from the bathroom without his disguise. It had been flawless; he had looked ten years older with greying sideburns and even eyebrows to match. The wig fitted perfectly and totally changed his appearance yet still looked completely natural.

It had taken several visits to a wee house in east Belfast which was Sammy's Auntie's house. Sammy was determined to have proper disguises when he conducted his surveillance tasks. His Aunty Mavis had been a makeup artist who had previously worked for the wardrobe department of the TVNI studios. It took hours of painstaking work to get the finished article. She had produced an excellent disguise.

He decided to try it out and even fooled his own wife and son when he met them one day in Belfast for lunch. He had taken a seat facing her in a café as they waited for him to arrive, not knowing he had been there the whole time. His wife even commenting to the son, 'That man keeps stirring at me.' She eventually decided to get up and leave as he was making her feel extremely uncomfortable. It was only then Sammy decided to identify himself to her. She commented even after knowing it was him, it was still creeping her out.

Sammy knew many a surveillance operative who had been caught out because of poor disguises or simply not having a suitable change of appearance. This was most evident when moving from different towns or cities. Surveillance aware targets would pick up on it.

Sammy himself remembered how when he was going through his surveillance training, he totally missed the hunched over aging man as he entered the library in Belfast. A covert meet between two targets had taken place within the building missed by the whole team and it was all down to the appearance change and disguises used.

He also remembered how he himself had detected surveillance being carried out against himself. One such episode was when he detected a female surveillance operative in Londonderry and again in Ballymena on one of his many surveillance operations. She had failed to make an appearance change and was seen wearing the same Laura Ashley styled dress in both locations. A simple mistake but a decisive error.

Kathy had played her part of loving wife and shopaholic well. It was a successful deception and one that should have at least for now satisfied Declan's interest in the Talbot family. The surveillance teams continued the task of shadowing Morag out of Dumfries before calling an end to their part of the operation, having already removed the tracker when she was in the shop.

The Talbot family were extremely grateful but had been deeply shaken by the whole experience. They had been told to remain in the house whilst Sammy and Kathy conducted their little charade at the shop. They had the extra security of the CP "close protection" guy. Peter had become quite agitated about their predicament. He turned to his Dad and said, 'They will not give up on hunting for us, at least not if O'Hara, Fox, and Greer were alive. You know those bastards are running the show over there.'

'How would you know they are running the show over there?' Sean asked, whilst at the same time dismissing his son's comment and not expecting an answer. It was a statement not lost on everyone present, but for now the potential compromise had been averted. The Talbot family could go back to life as before. Sammy could go home and relax having completed his contract in Afghanistan in support of the US government. Kathy could standdown once again.

Before Sammy left, he had a private chat with the Talbot family. He passed them a mobile number and stated that should the family feel they needed his help they should contact him on the number given.

'It is a burner phone and untraceable, at least it is not known by anyone else. Make sure you call from a phone box when using it. MI5 may still be monitoring all your registered numbers.'

Peter looked concerned by what he was hearing as he touched the small mobile in his pocket but said nothing.

'God forbid, but if they track you down they will show no mercy. You know the consequences for your actions against them. If what I heard from Kathy is correct and Declan O'Hara appears determined to hunt you down and they succeed in finding one or all of you, then my one piece of advice would be to demand to speak only to Declan. The security forces should be monitoring him in that given situation. It should provide some breathing space for you whilst Declan is sought and hopefully allowing time for the calvary to arrive.'

How serious they took his advice he didn't know but he knew the consequences of not taking it would not be pleasant.

Investigare

MI5 through GCHQ (Government Communication Headquarters) would continue to monitor the telephone traffic between Belfast and Glasgow post operation to be sure the threat to the Tierney's had been averted.

Chapter 13

Razor

Following the disappointment of the Dumfries operation and the unsuccessful identification of Steven Tierney, it was business as usual for the former IRA man. The landscape of Northern Ireland had changed so much following the signing of the Good Friday Agreement. For one, the release of more than five hundred prisoners from both sides of the religious or political divide was a hard pill to swallow for many and deemed a step too far for the victims of crime.

One of the effects of the Good Friday Agreement was it effectively made many members of the IRA redundant. Hence the reason many ex-members crossed to the dissidents.

***

Investigare

Razor was given a twenty-year sentence in the Maze for his part in the Oxford Street bombing in 1972. The incident being referred to as Bloody Friday. Razor had got his nickname because of the scar that stretched from his ear to the edge of his mouth. This was a result of a revenge attack following his rape of a young man in prison who later hanged himself.

On Razor's release he was confronted by the young man's father who attacked him with a razor blade as he stood at the bar in Sandy's. The father said he had been aiming to cut his throat but the interception by other men in the bar prevented him doing it properly.

Four weeks following the incident in the bar, the father was shot by a lone gunman as he walked his dog late at night. No one was ever convicted of the murder but word on the street was the not so good-looking Razor Fox was believed to be responsible for the man's death.

Razor Fox was a known pervert and deviant who liked nothing better than taking his aging, sagging, bulk of a body over to his favourite discreet and seedy massage parlour just off the Glen Road adjacent to the Christian Brothers School. One of several parlours in the area run by the dissidents. It was an extremely lucrative trade. The flow of women from the continent via the Republic was sponsored by criminal gangs. A small red candle in the upstairs window being the only indicator that behind the doors, two Asian women sharing the two-bedroom house were busy giving pleasure to their paying clients. The Asians were immensely popular since an Asian massage therapist was a familiar stereotype. Men were looking for something exotic, something different and the Asian women certainly provided that.

Razor's visit that night was expected as he was there for both business and pleasure. He was there for the collecting of rent or as it was better known, protection money. He would get his weekly relief from one or both ladies. Razor didn't care too much about what sex give the massage a masseur or masseuse and if there had been a male, he would still have enjoyed whichever of the sexes carried out his perverse massages if he got gratification with their happy endings.

Being bisexual only meant if Razor couldn't get it, then he would "bi" it. A joke he had repeatedly told to his so-called friends on several occasions and each time receiving the same disgusted look as a response.

It was Thursday and that meant Razor would be going to collect the weekly debt and take advantage of the massage therapists. The bedrooms which were used for the clients were pleasantly decorated with an oriental theme. Although there was a large bed within the room there was also a massage table. The ambient lighting helped in setting the tone which was created using dimmer switches for the lights. The music which was soothing and used as a soft background to help relax the paying guests was *a massage calm-soothing-water CD.*

The massage therapist would prefer using the bed when a client requested sex as the tables were there to add legitimacy to their massaging credentials. The tables were not popular with the women when the clients demanded sex as this would mean the massage therapist attempting sex acts on the narrow surface. This could lead to hilarious disaster or injury. Razor was no shrinking violet and the tables were far too narrow to accommodate large fat men and certainly not designed for performing sex on.

Razor had arrived just as a customer was exiting the property who was deliberately hiding his face as he passed Razor. Razor paused on the step in a moment of contemplation before turning his head back in the direction of the man and shouted, 'Don't worry Gerry Finnegan your secret is safe with me, I won't tell your wife.' Then laughed.

He entered the house closely watched by the stranger who was concealed in the grounds of the school.

'Right then ladies, business before pleasure,' he said. He took the envelope of money from the ladies and placed it inside his jacket before saying, 'Business seems good, just seen one of your clients leave maybe we will have to increase the rent.'

Both women looked at him with piercing eyes that were full of hatred before one said. 'You bad man, you get free fucky fucky and not nice.'

Razor laughed and said, 'Keep your knickers on, well at least for the minute and stop getting them in a twist we're good here, don't panic.'

He then made his way up the stairs grabbing the arm of one of the women.

'It's your lucky night Lee Ming,' he said as he almost dragged her behind him.

As he reached the landing, he heard the front door open then close again. *It is a busy night*, he thought.

Once in the room and even before he managed to get his coat off, he grabbed Lee Ming and pulled her tight up against his body. Placing his hands round her back and grabbing her backside but ensuring his fingers managed to find their way between her cheeks and into the crevice of her ass. Lee Ming pulled his hands away whilst saying,

'Not rough Razor, you too rough, please no hurt me that way.' Razor smiled and started removing his clothes whilst at the same time saying, 'I want a good hard massage and your lubricated finger in my butt. Then I want my cock placed through the hole on the table and you are going to give me the best blow job ever.'

Lee Ming was used to his deviant and perverted ways and this never shocked or fazed her. She just got on with the job at hand and was always grateful he left without her being hurt by him. Humiliation she could handle but his roughness she feared. Whenever he wanted sex on the bed it was always rough and always in the doggy position. He would pull her hair tight and yank her head back and the more she cried out for him to go easy, the harder he pulled. She was always grateful it only ever lasted a minute or so but she believed he got off on her cries rather than the sex.

On the table faced down with his limp dick positioned in the hole, Lee Ming started to apply the oils on his spotty back and pimpled ass. She had to climb on top of the table to ensure the correct pressure of massage could be applied but she was precariously balanced as his bulk took up almost the width of the table leaving very little room for her to place her knees.

As she massaged his body, he became more aroused with his dick hardening under the table. With his faced buried deep into the head rest, she continued massaging.

Investigare

The door to the room opened slightly and a figure standing in the entrance with their finger upright over the mouth indicating she be quiet. The figure holding a large knife in their other hand walked into the room and stealthily made their way over to the table. Lee Ming looked shocked as the stranger dressed in a hoody and balaclava indicated for her to climb off the table and come over.

Razor oblivious at this stage sensed Lee Ming climb down and mouthed, 'Make it a bloody good suck.'

The stranger indicated for her to do as she was told and climb under the table taking hold of his cock and placing it into her mouth. This was the first time she had ever done oral sex without the use of a condom as she was ill prepared and shaking like a leaf, not daring to take her eyes of the stranger. Razor gasped as she took his manhood in her mouth letting out a long satisfying sigh. At this point, the stranger stopped proceedings by indicating for Lee Ming to stop and climb out. As she was exiting from under the table Razor Shouted, 'What the fuck Lee, why have you stopped.' The stranger who was now beside the table reached down taking hold of the pulsating cock and with a quick slice of the knife, removed it. Lee Ming screamed and ran out the door.

Razor screamed and rolled onto his side as the blood shot out of the stub of a cock in spurts. He fell backward off the table onto the floor with a thud still holding the gash between his legs where his penis once swung. The stranger calmly walked around the table and stood over the top of the traumatised Razor brandishing the knife.

The removal of the balaclava sent chills through Razor's body on the realization he had seen the face of his torturer and executioner knowing he was going to die. Knowing time was limited the stranger knelt and staring into the eyes of the petrified Razor Fox forced the knife deep into his heart.

The penis was picked up of the floor and shoved into the mouth of Razor as a final act of ultimate humiliation. As the stranger left the room the balaclava was replaced. On passing the two women the stranger watched as Lee Ming was frantically trying to untie her fellow massage therapist. The stranger simply raised a finger over the mouth again indicating for the women to be silent and exited the house disappearing into the night.

***

The police arrived at the massage parlour on the Glen Road and discovered Razor Fox lying naked on the floor of the bedroom with his penis in his mouth and lying in a large pool of blood. Neither of the Asian women had dared go back into the bedroom. Lee Ming having witnessed the removal of Razor's penis by the hooded stranger was severely traumatised by the incident.

Both women were casualties of the trafficking and illegal sex trade made for lousy witnesses and were unable to provide any salient points worthy to assist the investigation. The women said that at no time had the perpetrator spoken but quietly went about their business with merciless efficiency. Both women having no formal identification claiming that their passports had long since been taken away from them by their captors. The women were taken into custody.

Once again, the police and the forensic team meticulously examined the crime scene. Fibres and several hairs were taken but considering how many people visited the massage parlour, the team wasn't confident anything to connect the perpetrator to the crime would be obtained.

Two murders of senior republicans' weeks apart, both with a knife as a murder weapon but until the autopsy was conducted, it was impossible to tell if it was the same weapon and therefore potentially the same perpetrator.

***

Declan was waiting for Razor to arrive with last night's takings when Micky Finn came into the house. In a raised high-pitched excited voice he said, 'Declan, Razor was murdered last night in the Glen Road parlour.' Micky appeared unconcerned; In fact, he came across as being happy to see the demise of the pervert.

'I can take over his run and look after the parlours if you want,' Micky said without thinking. The look on Declan's face told Micky he had overstepped the mark and not for the first time.

'Micky, I know you didn't fucking mean to sound so pitiless, so don't go getting above your station. You think you should be running the show here. Let's get one thing straight, you're the clown not the ring master and you better remember that. So don't be so fucking insensitive. If you're right and Razor is dead then we've just lost a good man.'

Micky realising, he had messed up tried to apologise by saying, 'I'm sorry Declan, I only meant to be helpful by offering to take on his role.' Declan just showed Micky the palm of his hand then waved him away as he needed to think about what had taken place.

Declan didn't like Micky, he had on more than one occasion been speaking behind Declan's back about the leadership and how he would run things if he were in charge. But Declan was very much aware as his men were loyal to him and had always told him to be weary of Micky. He reminded himself what Razor had told him, 'Keep your friends close but your enemy's closer.' So, Micky was always going to be at arm's length.

Declan intuitively knew that Micky was right though, it would be Razor who had been killed because for one, he was late and he was never late and two, he suspected one if not both the Asian women would have happily murdered him because he was a sadistic son of a bitch. Declan had heard stories of his sick and perverse habits and knew he was known to swing both ways and liked nothing better than when the Ladyboys show was in Belfast. Or as the old saying went, "Any port in the storm."

This was now the second member of the team to been murdered. Declan wondered if this could have been a robbery but it would have to be some sort of nutcase to steal money from him. Then he thought it could have been INLA trying to muscle in on their patch. Whatever the reason or whoever was responsible, it was certainly concerning. *Firstly, Teagan Greer and now Razor Fox. There were lots of new members and lots of fresh blood conducting republican business so what was there to be gained by getting rid of the old team. Maybe someone wants a bigger slice of the drug pie. It was a cutthroat business and Declan knew you needed to be ruthless to stay on top.* Something he had just reminded Micky Finn off.

***

Although the political landscape had changed in Northern Ireland, it had always been a fragile peace held together by appeasement and compromise to the republican agenda. Although Sinn Fein had convinced the IRA of their political goal to unify the island of Ireland, this wasn't enough for some and several members opted to join the New IRA or Dissidents. Not exactly original for the name change. Sinn Fein was now a hotbed of ex IRA members with the "Ex" being used extremely loosely.

The direction of the security service and the Police Service of Northern Ireland (PSNI) had been directed to the New IRA whose goal had always remained the unification of Ireland. They stated any border between Northern Ireland and the Republic of Ireland was a British border and therefore wouldn't be recognised.

The new IRA declaring themselves an army. They would continue to use the arms struggle to oppose any British infrastructure in the north and seek political and social change. Just the same rhetoric but different voices. No matter how it was portrayed it was still the same.

They haven't gone away you know.

Declan was at a loss trying hard to figure out why this was happening. *Why had two very close associates and ex senior Provo members been assassinated. This wasn't a coincidence, something sinister was taking place.*

Chapter 14

Declan's Fixation

Word was received back in Belfast that the hunt for Steven Tierney was unsuccessful following the visit to Dumfries and the Book Shop. Neither the owner or his English partner fitted the profile and as far as the Glasgow Cell was concerned that avenue of inquiry was finished. However, they promised they would continue in their pursuit of hunting down the family if this was Declan's desire.

Declan was disappointed by the result but he was still determined to find the tout Steven Tierney. He turned his attention to Tierney's family and in particular Rose and Paul.

Despite the passage of time his obsession on tracking the family had become so severe it was as if he had become haunted by the image of Steven Tierney laughing at him. He had been proven right all those years back when he made his case to the Provisional Army Council, stating that Tierney was a tout. Unfortunately, Tierney managed to escape his clutches before he had the chance to get him and Nutt him.

***

Declan visited Teresa Stitt at her home so he could ask if she knew of any reason or anyone that Rose Tierney could potentially still be in contact with in Belfast. The girls all knew each other back in the day and attended the same shebeens, bars and clubs but were never that close.

Teresa was surprised when he turned up at her door but even more taken aback by the time of day and his line of questioning. If she did have any information, she knew it would only put the Tierney family in trouble. Not that she had anything to add that could have been useful to him. She was the one that found the connection with Dumfries and had passed it on to Declan but the information turned out to be a dead end for which she was grateful.

Teresa let Declan into the house and showed him into the front lounge. She was still dressed in her dressing gown and wasn't best pleased he had called so early, particularly as it was Saturday and her day off.

Marie who had been upstairs when Declan arrived entered the living room wearing a large night shirt which barely covered her modesty but she appeared unconcerned by her appearance. Declan's head turned in her direction and looked at her a little too attentively before Teresa coughed to regain his attention. Marie lent back against the door frame and in doing so exposed a little more thigh than expected. It was clear Marie had been looking after herself in prison as even the exposed thighs were well toned and firm. There was a frosty moment between Declan and Marie.

Declan awkwardly asked Marie how she was doing? then stated, 'It's good to see you back home from…..' stumbling over the next word before Marie said, 'Prison, I think prison is the word you're looking for.'

'Well, you should be happy as I did you a favour,' said Marie.

'How so?' asked Declan.

'You probably got promoted didn't you when I killed that fucker Scrappy,' said Marie.

Teresa interjected before things got out of hand by saying to both, 'OK guys, let's be civil, no need to fall out here.'

Declan got up from his chair and said to Teresa, 'If you can think of anything or come across anything else from the computer, let me know. Oh, can I use the loo before I go?' he asked.

'Top of the stairs to the right,' Teresa said.

As Declan went up the stairs Marie said, 'I hate that fucker.'

'Shush,' he will hear you.

'I don't care.' she said, as she turned her head toward the stairs.

Declan made his way up the stairs passing the first of two bedrooms noticing the bed in the first room was neatly made whilst in the second, the bed was dishevelled. Declan give a wry smile to himself and felt a slight tingle in his groin. Once finished in the bathroom he returned downstairs giving a wry smile toward Teresa as he departed the hall and house.

'Wanker,' Marie said in his direction but not loud enough for him to hear, as he exited the house. If he did hear he never acknowledged.

Declan having no real avenue to explore with Rose turned his attention to the son.

Declan thought, *Paul would be in his twenties now but at 15 or 16 when the Tierney family left Belfast, he was still running around with lads his own age but lads that could potentially be helpful to him.*

Tig Francis was one such lad, he had been running errands for Declan and the dissidents for some considerable time now and had ingratiated himself to those people he believed were still IRA members in the area. Declan considered the lad a dependable volunteer. Although not a member of the dissidents himself or never having been Green Booked (recruited), he was still manipulated and used for various tasks. The delivery and collection of drugs being one such task. It had come to Declan's attention that he was part of a small group who ran around together back in their school era. Paul Tierney was also part of that grouping. *Maybe, just maybe they had not lost touch with each other* thought Declan, knowing he was still clutching at straws.

Declan had Tig Francis brought to him for a chat. On hearing he was to see Declan, Tig got overly excited as he knew he hadn't done anything wrong but thought, *this is it, I'm going up in the world maybe he will be giving me my own clients for the drugs.*

The conversation between the two was not what Tig had expected and he was confused that Declan was only interested in is youth and more importantly his time spent with his close friend at the time in Paul Tierney. Declan asked, 'Have you ever had any contact with Paul since he disappeared with his da?'

'Fuck no,' answered Tig, 'His da was a tout bastard and as far as I'm concerned so was he. I even told our Gina to have nothing to do with him.'

'What has Gina got to do with this Tig?' asked Declan.

'She had a thing for him, that's all, they went out together but I warned her that if he ever contacted her, she was to have nothing to do with him.'

'And did he?' asked Declan.

'Did he what?' said Tig.

Declan was starting to get infuriated and frustrated by this stage and being quite annoyed stated, 'Listen, if I wanted to listen to an asshole, I would fart myself. Raising his voice for the first time he said, 'Did Paul ever contact Gina for Christ's sake?'

'I don't know Declan, but I will ask her if you want.'

'Oh no no no …. You will do better than that, I want you to keep an eye on her and if you could get her mobile phone and check it for frequent numbers and get back to me with them.

'She's at college up in Derry and only comes home at weekends, well most weekends anyway.'

'Has she got a fella up there?' asked Declan

'Not that I'm aware off and she certainly hasn't brought anyone home here.'

'Right then young man, that will do for now. I need you to keep a close watch on your sister for me and report back anything you think might be important, is that understood.'

'Yes of course Declan,' said Tig.

Declan felt he might be clutching at straws, but every avenue needed to be explored and he was not getting any feedback from the Glasgow dissidents.

Chapter 15

Secret Liaisons

Peter walked off the Cairnryan to Larne ferry following its docking in the port of Larne. He had made the crossing as a foot passenger as he had done on several other occasions in the past. Waiting at the other side of the customs point was Gina Francis. The couple had taken it in turns to visit each other with Gina going across to Ayr in Scotland on just as many occasions as Peter had visited her in Northern Ireland. Peter had telephoned Gina a few months after his family's move to the mainland.

The two had remained friends and unknown to his parents had been going out with each other from their school days. It was a secret liaison and one which to date had remained so. The visits were always during holiday periods or weekends. They always hired a caravan either in Ayr in Scotland or up at Ballycastle on the Antrim coast for their secret get togethers. It was a major risk they were taking and one that could have so easily led to the compromise of his family.

Gina embraced Peter but immediately made the mistake as she stated, 'Oh Paul, I missed you.'

Peter looking around to ensure no one was in earshot said. 'Christ Gina It's Peter...Lord above.... we need to be careful.'

'Sorry...Its hard sometimes and I know...I'm sorry, God, I missed you.'

'Let's get out of here before someone sees us,' said Peter and they left the terminal building together.

On arrival at the carpark, Peter was taken aback when he saw Gina opening the door of a VW Beetle.

'Do you like the new wheels Pau.... Peter,' correcting herself.

'Well, it's not exactly discreet is it,' he said laughing. The bright yellow exterior and the large eye lashes on the headlights certainly made it stand out.

'If I wasn't worried about being discreet before, I am now.' Laughing he continued, 'let's get out of here Gina.'

Peter had always lied to his Ma and Da about his excursions stating he was spending time with a college friend in Ayr. They never suspected anything untoward was taking place.

Normally Peter and Gina would remain on the Caravan site so as not to be seen in public. They picked Ballycastle as Peter recalled that most of the catholic community from west Belfast normally went to Buncrana or up in Donegal for their holidays so he felt safe in Ballycastle. The protestants of the Shankill would normally go to the North Down coast to the popular resorts of Ballyhalbert or Millisle which was nicknamed "Shankill by the Sea."

Investigare

Gina was studying at Magee college Londonderry or as the city was often referred to, 'Stroke City' by the late radio presenter Gerry Anderson. Gina would bring Peter up to speed with all the goings on at home in the Ardoyne on their weekends together.

The feeling at the time of his family's disappearance was one of utter shock by many in the community. Apart from Gina's teenage broken heart of losing her boyfriend and months of not knowing where he was. The feeling of disappointment was something she couldn't shake. She questioned if Paul as he was known at the time knew of his dad's involvement.

When Gina received the first telephone call from Peter she was completely overwhelmed. The sudden surge of emotion from deep within her emanating in a guttural howl. It was like the sound of a wounded animal. She couldn't hold back the tears and emotion of relief.

Peter had said, 'Gina listen to me, you must never tell anyone about are telephone calls. If anyone finds out, I will be dead and so will my Ma and Da. Swear to me you will never tell anyone, swear it, Gina, swear it now.'

'I swear it, Paul.'

'Don't ever call me that, its Peter. From now on Paul is dead, it's Peter now. You must call me Peter.'

'Ok, I've got it…Peter.'

'But I don't even know where you're Living.'

'I can't tell you that, you will just have to trust me on this.'

Gina now believed it must be Scotland because of the convenience of their rendezvous but she never pressed him further on the matter. Their relationship had developed slowly over the years and as young lovers do, they even considered eloping and getting married at Gretna Green.

The time spent together was dangerous but they believed they were taking every precaution possible to avoid being compromised. Peter had to learn fast following his move and was well coached about his security and how to be astute by the security service team. Peter and Gina continued their clandestine liaisons together. All that remained now to was to get back home having spent another romantic weekend together without raising the suspicions of his parents.

Chapter 16

Marie's Nightly Excursions

Marie had been staying in Teresa's house ever since being released from prison. The two girls had been getting on well. What had started as a bit of flattery between the girls and something that had always been instigated by Marie was developing into something more than friendship.

When Marie first arrived in the house she would walk about in her bra and pants which Teresa had to admit to herself, Marie was still an incredibly attractive and seductive woman. She would flaunt her body in front of Teresa. Teresa tried to justify it as Marie's prison experience and her having no inhibitions about her body. But she knew she was being slowly seduced and it excited her.

They slept in separate bedrooms at least initially but as time went on, they eventually moved into the one bed. During a night in and having consumed a little too much wine, they ended up sitting on the settee facing each other with their glasses of wine in hand discussing each other's hang-ups. It was Marie who started by stating the kiss at the gates of the prison was an innocent action but she had noticed the reaction was one of acceptance by Teresa.

Teresa tried to justify her reaction stating, 'It was one of shock, but I didn't read anything into it.'

Marie, responded by saying, 'I notice how you look at me as I walk about the house, and I've experienced that look many times in prison. So, I know you like what you see.' Teresa's heart was racing so fast and was pounding on her chest so hard, she felt it would burst at any minute.

'You have slept with other women before haven't you,' asked Marie.

'No…Yes…., I mean once at college, but it was only a drunken one-night thing.'

'But did you enjoy it? asked Marie.

Teresa was blushing so much, she felt herself go weak and giddy. Marie reached across and took Teresa's free hand firmly but tenderly in hers. Setting her glass on the coffee table she gently stroked the side of Teresa's face, running the tip of her finger down and across her lips before sliding the finger into her mouth.

Teresa responded by gently sucking on the finger as she slowly rotated her tongue around it. Marie removed her finger and continued with the finest of touches over her chin and down her neck. Teresa became totally subservient to the touches. Her body was covered in goosebumps as every nerve receptor was being stimulated with the tender caressing.

Leaning forward Marie kissed her fully on the mouth. A long and seductive kiss and one Teresa didn't want to end. She could taste the wine on her lips and smell the intoxicating aroma of her perfume and it was delicious.

The kiss got deeper and more passionate and Teresa wanted her so badly. She felt a burning desire that was being lit deep inside her. Not even at college did she feel such an imploring desire for more.

The two women became entangled in each other as their bodies moved in harmony exploring every inch of each other. Marie placed her firm toned thigh between the legs of Teresa as their bodies moved in unison. It was all that was needed to bring Teresa to climax. Eventually the two women retired up the stairs to Teresa's room and continued their night of passion.

***

Teresa was still mindful of the arrest of Marie following the murder of Teagan Greer and her part in providing an alibi for her close friend. She couldn't shake the feeling that Marie was hiding something from her. She kept trying to put it out of her mind but every so often it would eat at her. Teresa couldn't help but wonder why Marie had lied about her whereabouts on the night of Teagan's murder. As much as she tried to trust her friend, doubts nagged at the back of her mind. What else had Marie been hiding? and why? They had always been honest with each other, so this secrecy was unnerving. Teresa replayed their countless conversations since Marie's arrest, searching for any hints or inconsistencies that she might have missed. But everything seemed normal, making her even more frustrated.

The two women continued to socialise together in Sandy's bar. Teresa was mindful of Marie's past and the issues she previously had in Sandy's with it being an IRA haunt and her having killed one of their members. So, Teresa was reluctant to go there but it was Marie who was adamant she was not hiding away and wanted to go.

Marie commented that the place hadn't changed one bit whilst she was away. The two girls were quietly sitting drinking and listening to songs from the pop idol wannabees on the Karaoke machine when the republican and one of Declan's men, Kevin Moore entered the bar. He went straight to the counter and ordered a pint. He looked around the bar and on seeing the girls, he raised his pint glass into the air mouthing, Slainte, (Cheers in Irish). Marie who was sitting with her back to him was unaware anything had happened until Teresa lifted her own glass and said, 'That's Kevin Moore saying hello.' Marie slowly turned her head in the direction of the man who by now was facing back toward the bar. 'Is it indeed,' being her only reply, as she stirred intently at the man at the bar.

During the evening, Marie had become distant and quiet with Teresa asking her, 'Are you alright Marie?' Her mood had changed she appeared not to be enjoying the quiet drink with her friend any longer.

'Teresa, do you mind if we go now, I'm not feeling great and these idiots screaming into the microphone are giving me a headache. The girls downed their drinks and exited the bar. Teresa waved in the direction of Kevin but Marie remained focused on the exit totally ignoring the man keeping her body turned to the side as if to avoid him.

Once back at the house, Teresa put the kettle on with the intention of making both girls a hot drink. Marie appeared at the kitchen door still with her coat on and stated,

'I'm going to go out for a walk as I need to get some fresh air in the hope of ridding myself of this headache' she had claimed to have. 'Wrap up warm,' Teresa said, 'it's so much colder now at nights.' With that Marie exited the house and into the night.

***

Declan had just left the late-night café across from one of his drug dens on the Glen Road. As he stepped outside the door and started to button up his coat to fend off the bitterly cold breeze, he was debating whether to go to Sandy's for a pint before returning home for the night when the shot rang out. He could see the flash of the gun barrel from across the street, followed by the crack and thump as the bullet smashed into the door of the café beside him.

He managed to fall back against the door forcing it open as he desperately tried to seek cover from within. A second round had been heard as he was still taking cover.

He managed to push the door close with his feet. He immediately checked he hadn't been hit by running his hands over his body at the same time screaming at the over tanned waitress to turn the lights off. He was sure he could just make out the shape of a figure across the street at the time of the shooting.

Within minutes the police arrived at the scene and two empty cartridges were found in the entry from where the shots had been fired. As he was being interviewed, an over excited Micky Finn arrived at the café, forcing his way past the police toward Declan. 'Christ, I just heard you were shot at. Thank God you're all right. Any idea who did it.' Not waiting for an answer, he turned to the nearest police officer and stated, 'I bet it was you lot, or one of your loyalists hired guns.'

Chapter 17

Tig

Gina Francis was at home on a half term break from college and Tig was not slow in plundering through her personal possessions whenever the opportunity presented itself. Getting hold of her mobile was a bit more problematic as it was always in her hand. *I think the bloody thing is glued to her hand,* he surmised.

Tig was keen to impress Declan and if he could gain favour by exposing his sister then he would do whatever it took. He managed to find her diary and having locked himself in the bathroom started to read his sisters most intimate memoirs. Although embarrassed by what he was doing, he took a guilty pleasure in reading her most private thoughts that she had placed down on paper.

As he carried out his duplicitous task with Gina's diary, he came across several entries which referred to weekends with P. One entry which read, *"Being cozied up in the caravan with "P" rapped in each other's arms as we listened to the crashing of the waves on the rocks. Time I never want to end but know he must eventually go and I must stay. I will be left counting the days until we are together again."* She had started and finished her entry with a small heart with a pierced arrow with the letters G and P on either side of it within the heart.

He flicked through the pages and there had been several of these entries but it was only these that displayed the heart. As he flicked over the empty pages, he came across another blank page but at the top was the heart and the inscribed G & P but no other entry other than the date of 20th June.

***

Tig visited Declan to report his findings from his unscrupulous task against his sister. He was unable to gain access to Gina's phone as it was never any further than arms reach from her.

'So, what have you to report,' asked Declan.

'Well, she is seeing someone and has been spending time with him several weekends according to her diary,' said Tig.

'Does she mention her fella by name,' Declan asked.

'No, she just has initials of G and P in her diary but that could be anybody, even someone from college' Tig informed Declan, He continued; 'It would appear she spends time in a caravan but there is nothing to indicate where that is.'

'You're a clever lad Tig Francis, it could be nothing but I need you to continue spying on your wee sister and keep me informed. I could do with a good smart lad like yourself around here, said Declan knowing he was playing on the lads' ego.

Tig was delighted, and responded by saying, 'I just want to help,' then continued, 'Oh, she has an entry in her diary for the 20th of June. I know that is the end of term for her but the date is highlighted in her diary.'

'Does she stay on campus at Magee or has she got student digs,' asked Declan.

'No, she stays in a bedsit with other students, maybe one of them is this P,' said Tig.

'Do you know the address Tig?'

'No, but she said she lived near the college. I can find out easily enough as my Dad paid her deposit and he will have paperwork.'

'Good lad, if you get anything else, I want you to get back to me right away.'

***

Following the conversation with Tig, Declan had managed to achieve the confirmation needed of Gina's address on Rock Road. The property was just a few hundred yards from the Strand Road police station but still convenient for the college. Declan called another member of his team, Jim Carlin and told him he had a future assignment for him. Although the 20$^{th\ of}$ June was still over a month away, Declan wanted to make sure Jim had a chance to conduct a recce of Magee college and the surrounding area. It may have been a long shot but if there was a possibility that Paul Tierney was in country then he wanted to speak with him.

***

A trip to Derry was arranged with a safe house being organised for an overnight stay by a leading republican in the city. Following a night out in The Bellstar bar with fellow republicans, Jim was taken to a house in the Creggan Estate on Malin Gardens where he was shown into a house.

The front door was on the latch as he entered and went directly up the stairs to a back bedroom which had been prepared for his stay. As he went up the stairs he could see into the living room and a family seated watching TV but paying him no attention.

The republican movement had several of these safe houses scattered across the city with the occupants extremely willing to help the cause. Jim was up and away early the next morning to Magee college Campus before any members of the family were up and about.

It didn't take long to track down Gina or her recently acquired new VW Beetle. A trip to her bedsit on Rock Road highlighted she was sharing with two other girls. So at least that ruled out a boyfriend she may have been shacked up with. He spent a few hours tailing her as she and her flat mates went into town but this was deemed a waste of time as the girls spent the time going around shops. Having obtained all that was needed,

Investigare

Jim returned to Belfast and back briefed Declan on his findings. A plan of action was conceived for the 20th ^{of} June when Jim would again return to Derry and place Gina Francis under surveillance.

Chapter 18

Band of Brothers

Sammy had settled back into life at home in Northern Ireland and continued his rigorous fitness regime. He prided himself as always being ready for deployment to some troubled hotspot at a moment's notice.

He was back at the helm of his surveillance and investigation company. It was a reliable source of income for him and his men when not deployed elsewhere on their bogus adventures.

A team of three men having had ample experience in surveillance operations from their time in the forces made it a natural choice of employment to undertake. Sammy had several ex-police and army personnel on the books so it was easy to get cover for their absences.

The real money was in the overseas contracts so, the insurance fraud claims or medical negligence work was treated as small fry for pocket money when they were at home between their operational commitments.

Investigare

***

Davy had served in Northern Ireland on several operational tours before completing selection for the SOG "Special Operations Group," a covert military unit conducting counter insurgency operations against the paramilitary groupings. It was during such operations he worked in cooperation with Special Branch and the HMSU. It was here that he became good friends with Sammy. Davy was originally from Arbroath Scotland and was an ex-member of the Special Boat Service (SBS) of the Royal Marines.

Following the Good Friday Agreement and the withdrawal of the Army from province, Davy moved to the newly formed DHU (Defence Humint Unit) and its Alpha Detachment which was responsible for worldwide Human Intelligence operations. Having completed several tours of duty in IRAQ and Afghanistan, he decided the frequency of tours was becoming boring and mundane, so he left the forces and joined a network of Special Forces colleagues on the Close Protection Circuit (CP).

He had deployed all over the world guarding notable people such as footballers and pop stars, Saudi Princes, and several foreign dignitaries. The call from Sammy asking him if he would come and work in a small nit team of surveillance specialists with each member having an excellent understanding of the demographics and a sound geographical knowledge of

Northern Ireland was just too good an opportunity to turn down. It would reunite the Band of brothers again with Sammy and a third member and close friend Roy.

***

Roy the third member of Sammy's team grew up in Kesh in Fermanagh. A beautiful small village which set at the north-western end of the wonderful scenic Lough Erne with its breathtaking views. Roy would always say 'For six months of the year the lakes were in Fermanagh but the other six, Fermanagh was in the lakes.'

His family had what would have been considered a medium sized farm with several acres close to Donegal. Roy had been away at college when his father a farmer and local councillor was murdered whilst working the fields of the farm.

The IRA had planted an IED just inside a gate entrance to one of his fields. As he crossed the cattle grid into the field on his small Massey Ferguson tractor the two faceless terrorists watched in silence as their callous and murderous operation was about to come to fruition. Both hidden from view, they prepared themselves for the outrage and chaos that would soon follow.

As Roy's father went about his business, he was oblivious to the imminent danger. He was completely unaware of the threat that loomed over him. His only concern that day was tending to his land, providing food for his family and the community.

Investigare

With a sense of finality, one of the terrorists pushed the button on a remote detonator, triggering the deadly device they had planted. In an instant, a violent explosion ripped through the air, shattering the peaceful quiet of the countryside. The force of the blast consumed the tractor and its operator, robbing the farmer of his life in a matter of seconds.

They had achieved their goal, a sickening victory in their twisted ideology. Their violent act had taken the life of an innocent man. As the echoes of the explosion faded away, the field stood as a haunting testament to the destructive power of hatred and extremism.

Roy's father had been an independent councillor, he had no political affiliation and worked tirelessly for his constituents from both sides of the religious divide. At that time intimidation was ripe with many of the unionist community being threatened and forced to sell up their homes and land.

It was systematic ethnic cleansing of the border regions. This process continued over the years with a demographic switch of population. The unofficial new border being thirteen miles further north of Rosslea at Fivemiletown.

The death of his father was all the motivation Roy needed to join the RUC. It was not to seek retribution but rather he wanted to protect society from the evils that lurked in all the paramilitary groupings. He worked in uniform before making the move into the specialist elite unit of HMSU. As a member of HMSU he had many close encounters and assassination attempts against him. He did however manage to get Justice for his father's death on the perpetrators and cowardly killers.

The same two IRA men responsible for his father's death were caught in the act of another assassination attempt on yet another member of the armed forces. This time it was against another farmer who was also a part time member of the UDR (Ulster Defence Regiment), he would spend his days working on the farm just as Roy's own father had done but he would spend several evenings each week helping to protect his community by patrolling the border and its many illegal crossing points into the republic.

The two IRA men who were brothers and known as the "Fermanagh Twin Bombers" were in the process of placing a device under the soldier's car when it went off prematurely killing both men.

**

Sammy, Davy, and Roy had worked together on numerous different contracts since leaving the police and military but were in the early planning stage of yet another deployment. This time it was to be Sierra Leone and the fight against the West Side Boys. An armed terrorist group who were sometimes described as a splinter faction of the Armed Forces Revolutionary Council.

Sammy had been deployed in Afghanistan when he heard about Operation Barrasa.

Operation Barrasa was a British Army operation that took place in Sierra Leone on 10 September 2000, during the latter stages of the nation's civil war. The operation was to release captured British soldiers of the Royal Irish Regiment and their Sierra Leone Army liaison officer, who were being held by a militia group.

The soldiers were part of a patrol that was returning from a visit to Jordanian peacekeepers attached to the United Nations Mission in Sierra Leone (UNAMSIL). The patrol of twelve men were overwhelmed by many heavily armed rebels and taken prisoner. Sammy's old Regiment the Para's along with the SAS were sent on the rescue mission to free the captured troops.

The three men intended to go on their mentoring mission to Sierra Leone and help mentor the Intelligence community of the government forces.

All three men had become close friends and believed to get justice then you had to fight fire with fire and none of them would lose any sleep in carrying out their covert and deceptive tasks if that was what was needed.

On Sammy's return from Dumfries, he got the team together and briefed them on the circumstances of the Talbot family and the relentless pursuit by Declan O'Hara to hunt them down. Each man was in total agreement that they should get proactive and work against O'Hara and his men.

Chapter 19

Operation Phone Hack

'Has Fred at DDT, (Deep Dive Technology) been told what is expected of him and when,' asked Sammy.

'Yes, but maybe not when, but he knows what we want and he is on standby,' said Davy.

DDT was created by a team of technicians who worked for Special Operations Group (SOG) an intelligence agency and were all experts in the field of telecommunications. They were particularly brilliant at code breaking and deep diving into the dark web. They were especially skilled at hacking equipment. Anything to do with cyber technology, security and accessing data was very much their bread and butter. They also had the contracts for the supplying of listening devices, camera both overt and covert to the Ministry of Defence for Special Forces use.

Fred had been instrumental in the provision of such devices for the Unit which were used against several of the terrorist organisations over the years.

Investigare

Sammy had already been privileged to the Special Branch Intelligence Report (SBIR) and the Signal Intelligence Reports (SIGINT) from the communications centre concerning the Tierney case when he was in Dumfries. The telephone numbers contained in the reports pertaining to Declan O'Hara and Jock McClean were noted and saved by Sammy. Fred the CEO of DDT would be able to track these numbers which was exactly what Sammy had hoped for.

On his return from Dumfries, Sammy had decided Sean would never be safe if Declan and Co continued their pursuit of him. So, Sammy and the team had already started their own background work against the terrorist grouping.

Following a conversation with Fred at DDT, Sammy was told if he could produce any telephone numbers of the ASU then he could help him keep tabs on all the main players. As it was, it worked out to be a stroke of genius. The consequence of this action would pay dividends further down the road. The three men had already started directing operations against the terrorist group.

One such operation was to obtain the telephone number for Jim Carlin. The team had originally deployed to Carlin's home just off the Glen Road in Divis Drive. Having moved into pre-planned positions, Davy was able to have overwatch of the targets home and observe his movements. The positions taken by the team effectively boxed off the area making certain whichever direction he went; an operator would be able to follow either on foot or mobile.

Davy was parked on Divis Drive just short of the junction with Norbury street facing south back toward the main road. The other two operators Sammy and Roy had taken positions covering the main transit routes out onto the Glen Road. Divis Street only had houses on one side as Translink bus servicing depot ran the full length of the other side with its large wall and corrugated fencing. This give a natural cover as numerous workers from Translink would park their cars alongside the wall.

It had been raining that morning and was still extremely overcast in the city. Davy was observing Carlin's house when he heard voices coming from the direction of the Falls Park playing fields situated directly behind him. On taking a quick glance in the rear-view mirror he could see six men in paramilitary style jackets, balaclavas and carrying an assortment of weapons from AK47's, an RPG-2 anti-tank "Rocket Propelled Grenade" launcher and pistols. Not having a lot of time to react, he lowered himself the best he could whilst at the same time managing to get across into the passenger footwell.

He pulled his jacket from the seat and dragged it across his body ensuring his face wasn't totally exposed but allowing a small gap from which he could still see. He then made himself as small as possible keeping his body up tight against the passenger door. He held his Walther PPW in his hand and waited. He managed to radio the team as to what was taking place. Knowing that any movement now in the form of a hasty getaway would have resulted in the terrorists opening fire on the car as it made its escape.

He couldn't be sure if there was still members of the gang behind him should he need to make a rapid withdrawal on foot toward the park. All he could do was wait out the presence of the terrorists and hope for the best.

Two terrorists walked past his vehicle, one on either side of the car but fortunately they were busy talking to each other which meant they would have been looking across the top of the car rather than paying any attention to the interior. As he watched the terrorists walk past, a sense of relief washed over him. Their casual demeanour and preoccupation with their conversation may have unknowingly spared him from detection. His vehicle blended seamlessly with the surroundings, just another parked car on that side of the street.

Inside the car, he kept his breathing steady, maintaining his composure. The situation was precarious, and he knew any sudden movement or noise could shatter the illusion of inconspicuousness.

As they passed, he couldn't help but notice the calculated yet shared paranoia in their eyes. Davy believing, they were on a mission, focused on whatever sinister plot they had set in motion, oblivious to the ordinary world around them.

The terrorists set up an Illegal Vehicle Checkpoint done in a show of strength about twenty meters in front of Davy's vehicle. They remained in position for about twenty minutes before quickly exiting back up Divis Street and onto the playing fields of the Falls Park. *The public bar McSwain's at the bottom of the Street most likely had a lookout in the upstairs window ready to warn the terrorists of any approach by the police,* thought Davy.

Sammy did a drive pass of Davy's vehicle reporting the area was now free from the terrorists. Davy had stated that if any of the terrorists had glanced in through the rain-stained passenger window with any degree of awareness, he could have been compromised. It was a frightening and an extremely long twenty minutes. Davy reflected on the incident and knew that despite the numerous lessons learnt from previous dangerous scenarios he had found himself in, this could have ended very differently.

He thought back to the shocking images that were broadcast around the world of the two Army corporals who had been dragged from a car they had been travelling in and murdered only a matter of a few hundred meters away from his current location. He knew had he been pulled from the car by the terrorists there was a real possibility of it ending in his death. Although he also knew, he would have a much better chance of surviving the situation as he had back up with Sammy and Roy.

Regardless, he knew with certainty he would have taken several of the terrorists with him. The adrenaline rush he experienced during the twenty minutes was such that his heart rate increased significantly, yet he had a professional level of calmness and situational awareness that one could only achieve with the years of operational experience he had.

Shortly after the show of strength by the dissidents Carlin exited his house. Roy left his car and followed Carlin on foot closely watched by Davy and Sammy.

Following Jim Carlin had been routine for the team. Roy and Davy took it in turns to conduct the surveillance of Carlin on foot whilst Sammy remained mobile as back up should a quick extraction of the men be needed. Having left his house on

Investigare

the Glen Road, he made his way to Donnelly's Newsagents and picked up his Irish News tabloid.

He then went directly to Brenda's Diner for breakfast. A routine he consistently repeated during surveillance of him. This morning was no different. Davy wondered if the man had ever used a cooker except for when torturing someone.

Davy entered the café and walked past the glass fronted sandwich bar and set in a seat toward the rear of the room. The café had six small tables with yellow and white chequered plastic tablecloths. These were the colours of the Antrim Gaelic football team. They played in nearby Casement Park.

Each table had a set of condiments consisting of bottles of red and brown sauces and small metal sugar bowls containing both white and brown sugar sachets. There was a mix of two and four wooden chairs parked at each table. Davy positioned himself at a two-seater table with his back to the wall giving him a complete overview of the whole space, this being a fundamental surveillance must.

The small, cramped kitchen was in full swing to his right with the smell of fried food emanating from it. As greasy spoons went this fitted the bill perfectly and a good fry up could be guaranteed.

Jim Carlin was a lone figure seated near the front window tucking into his fry. Having ordered a tea and bacon bap from the young girl with her fake tan which looked like it had been applied by a paint roller. It was clearly put on without the use of surgical gloves as the palms of her hands were so badly stained. It looked streaky, patchy, and bright orange. A tin of Ronseal from Homebase would have worked better. It clearly didn't have the desired effect the young girl had wished for and it certainly wasn't a perfect sun-kissed look.

Davy continued to observe Carlin greedily shovelling his fry. Once he had finished devouring his food, he opened his paper and started to read whilst gulping down his large mug of tea. Davy wanting to get Jim's attention was making grunting noises of aggravation and frustration whilst holding his mobile telephone in the air and swearing whilst complaining about the poor signal quality.

Carlin looked up at Davy and asked, 'Are you having problems.'

'Can't seem to get a bloody signal in here, have you got a signal mate.'

Carlin took his phone out of his jacket pocket then punched in his code to unlock it and checked, 'Yeah no problem, full bars.'

'Maybe it's the network,' stated Carlin.

'Could be,' said Davy.

Carlin then said, 'Who are you with?' then continued without waiting on the answer, 'I'm with 3 and its good coverage.

'Friggin Tesco mobile, never again,' responded Davy.

'Carlin then placed his phone on the table which was what Davy had been hoping for.

Fred at DDT had placed the cloning device on Davy's phone and if he was in line of sight to Carlin's phone, then he could retrieve the information he wanted. It would only take a matter of seconds and everything held on the phone would be cloned.

Investigare

Davy had his phone on silent when he received a text telling him the task had been successful and he could leave when ready.

Fred at DDT received the number displayed on his computer screen.

Davy then turned to the Belisha Beacon of a waitress and asked if he could have his bacon roll to go as he needed to get outside to get a signal. He thanked Carlin again who was back engrossed in his Irish News and exited the café.

Chapter 20

The Stranger

The stranger had been watching the house in Lenadoon and had been observing the comings and goings at the property by Bap Quinn and his cohorts.

The house was situated on the end of a terrace row. All the properties had three bedrooms with a kitchen to the back of the house and lounge at the front. Each property in the row had a small front garden and yard to the rear. The house the stranger was watching, the front garden had long since gone, being replaced by broken flag stones providing a makeshift driveway.

During the stranger's observations it was noted that one of the cohorts who had entered the property was observed leaving through a house four doors down on the same row.

The stranger had been observing the front of the properties but wondered if by some chance this individual had exited the rear of one property and went through another to avoid detection. The stranger believing it was done for added security reasons. It had not dawned on the stranger that several properties had holes made within the roof spaces between each of the properties. This was done to aid ASU members make their escape following shooting attempts on the Army and Police patrols in the area.

Consideration by the security forces was always given to observing the roof tops as they patrolled looking for any tell-tale signs of displaced tiles and such, thus possibly identifying a shooting position. It was common for a small roof tile to be moved just enough for a barrel of a gun to shoot through. You could guarantee whichever house you identified the shooter to be firing from was not the house he or she would be exiting from.

The gap in the attic walls allowed the shooter or shooters to crawl between attics and make good their escape. The army always split into bricks or four-man teams and moved up both sides of the street covering each other whilst providing protection for police to conduct their tasks. It was standard practice for each patrol to be accompanied by one or two police officers.

***

The last of the day's sunlight was quickly disappearing as the sun was going down behind Divis mountain when the same cohort returned to the property in a dark blue Volvo Estate. It was parked on the driveway and backed up close to the front door.

The driver was joined by two other men at the front door who appeared to be carrying something large and bulky rapped in a carpet from inside the house. The first thought of the stranger was *it had to be a body.* Once the item was placed in the rear of the vehicle all three men left the property in the car. The stranger noticed Bap Quinn had appeared briefly in the doorway as the vehicle exited the property and the street.

The stranger who had been observing the comings and goings for some considerable time, had recognised all four men during that time but one was conspicuous by his absence as he was the odd one out today.

Christ, the stranger thought, *it was at the massage parlour on the Glen Road when tracking Fox at the man was noted leaving. The stranger remembered how the man's name was called out by Razor when he shouted after him, 'Gerry your secret is safe with me, I won't tell your wife.'* Now the stranger believed that it must be Gerry in the boot of the car. *Well, it certainly wasn't a carpet being dumped,* the stranger thought.

Knowing that everyone but Bap had already left the house the stranger went round to the rear of the property and entered the back yard. The bins were overflowing and rubbish was discarded everywhere. It was a complete pit. An old washing machine had been discarded with its door having been ripped off and tossed several feet away against the wall.

The stranger was mindful not to step in cat droppings that also littered the yard. The stranger knocked at the back door and waited for it to be answered by Bap. It was the stranger's intention to act fast and as soon as the door was opened, rush Bap taking him by surprise.

Investigare

    Dressed in a hoodie and wearing a balaclava the stranger barged through the door knocking Bap backwords making him slip and fall on the wet floor. This making it easier to overpower the man. Bap had landed on his back on the floor, his head colliding against the hard kitchen surface.

    As he fell he knocked over the mop bucket spilling its contents all over the kitchen floor. Before Bap had a chance to recover, the stranger was on top of him straddling Bap's body brandishing a large knife whilst trying to thrust it into his chest.

    Bap struggled with the stranger on the wet floor whilst the stranger still brandishing the knife with one hand trying desperately to stab Bap in the chest. Bap was resisting by taking hold of the stranger's wrist whilst at the same time trying to retrieve the pistol from his waistband, eventually managing to bring it round in his right hand.

    Still struggling to defend himself against the stranger, he tried to turn the gun in the direction of his assailant. With a quick thrust of the knife, the stranger managed to cut across the wrist of Bap, resulting in him firing two shots which went up through the ceiling of the kitchen. As the blood spurted from the gash on his wrist, he cried out in pain as the knife was plunged deep into his heart. As blood was coming out of his mouth as he grasp for his last breaths, the stranger removed the balaclava to ensure Bap would see the face of his killer.

    Out of breath and close to exhaustion the stranger wiped the knife on the chest of Bap. Conscious of being sprayed with Bap's blood, the stranger cleaned off as much as possible before exiting back out of the rear door, quicky making progress along the alleyway back onto the main road.

The stranger knew there was a woman in the house but during the surveillance she had always been observed upstairs and could be seen pacing back and forward past the bedroom and landing windows.

***

It was a full twenty-four hours before the police went to the house following an anonymous phone call. On arrival at the property, DS Ken Stones from the Serious Crime Unit arrived and observed the body of Bap Quinn on the kitchen floor. However, what he also found was a female dead in the back bedroom. She had been shot in the back as she lay asleep on the bed. The house had been secured to allow the CSI team to conduct their expert recovery of evidence from the scene.

'So, what's the verdict Barry,' asked DS Stones of the senior forensic officer in charge.

'You're not going to like it Ken,' responded Barry, then continued, 'It looks like we have a serial killer on our hands.' No detective likes to hear the words 'serial killer.' Ken knew the sense of panic from the public would be immense if that got out.

Most murders are normally carried out in a moment of rage or passion, but these three murders had all the hall marks of paramilitary involvement and god knows Ken Stones had seen enough of them over the years. Both murders may have been similar in their Modus Operandi, yet they were unorthodox in every way. But as twisted as the killer and murders may seem, Ken knew even at this early stage of the investigation it was drugs and paramilitary involvement behind it.

'What about the lady upstairs?' asked Ken.

'It was a round fired through the ceiling by Bap Quinn that killed her. Gunshot residue has been found on his hand. There was clearly a fight or struggle that took place. Although, it may take a few days to establish, but once the autopsy is completed you will find its probably the same knife that had been used in two previous murders, Teagan Greer, and Razor Fox,' said Barry.

It was Ken who continued with his thoughts on the matter by stating, 'Despite someone's best attempts at scrubbing the kitchen table and floor, which was probably your wee man lying there, I think you'll find the DNA from blood and brain matter on the kitchen table will match that of Gerry Finnegan whose body we found late last night in an alleyway in a very badly staged drug robbery.' He continued, 'A vehicle only partially burnt out near the west link had been recovered and taken in for the forensic team to go over. Once again, I'm sure DNA recovered will implicate some members of the Lenadoon drug gang,' a confident DS Stones concluded.

Chapter 21

Follow the Beetle

Jim Carlin accompanied by another volunteer Joe Byrne travelled up to Londonderry on the evening of the 19th. Having confirmed the presence of the VW Beetle outside the Rock Road bedsit, they took up a position to watch the parked car and observe the comings and goings at the property.

Joe left Jim in the car observing the bedsit and walked the short distance back up the Strand Road to McDonalds for food for the two men. Whilst away from the car, Gina Francis exited the bedsit with a small suitcase. Jim Carlin felt a surge of panic as his partner in crime was still away getting the refreshments. The thought of having to leave him if Gina drove off from the bedsit filled him with dread. Christ, he thought, *how would I explain that to Declan.*

Joe had just turned back into Rock Road when he also had seen Gina coming down the steps of the elevated front door of the old Victorian bedsit. He panicked and dropped the bag containing the burgers, chips and two coffees. Having sworn aloud having burnt his hand on the hot spilled coffee he drew the attention of Gina Francis as she looked in his direction she could see a man stoop down to retrieve whatever it was he had dropped.

Joe realising what had happened ensured his back was to Gina as he bent down.

Gina turned back to her car placing the case into the back seat. Locking the car, she looked down the road but the man had gone. She then returned in doors.

Joe came back out from behind the car from which he had taken cover. With a crumpled bag of food, he made his way back to Jim.

No further movement was observed at the bedsit except for the lights going out just after eleven that evening. The two men took it in turns to watch the bedsit through the night. Jim told Joe about the suitcase getting put in the car. He believed it was just to save time in the morning. He then instructed Joe not to take his eyes of the car in case she left in the early hours during his watch.

At 7:45am Gina exited the bedsit down the steps to her car. She was in possession of what Jim thought looked like a makeup bag or holdall as she got into the car. She was alone and travelled out of Londonderry by crossing the Craigavon bridge to the waterside, then travelled onto Limavady, Coleraine, Ballymoney, Ballymena and eventually arriving Larne harbour ferry port by 9:30am. She had made good timing despite a brief stop in Ballymena for a takeaway coffee and a breakfast bap.

A very tired Jim Carlin telephoned Declan and informed him of the proceedings thus far and briefed him of the expected arrival of the Cairnryan ferry which was due to dock at 10:00am according to the large neon sign outside the terminal. He stated, 'It appears Gina is here to pick someone up as she is not in the departure carpark or lanes.'

Declan was delighted by the news and said, 'Jim make sure you let me know once she had met up with whoever it is she is expecting.'

The car containing the two occupants was easy recognisable due to it being bright yellow with large decorative eye lashes. The exit from the port was easily observed as was the occupants of the vehicle. Jim Carlin turned to Joe and said,

'That's our boy.'

'Are you sure? asked Joe the driver.

'One hundred percent, he's the spit of his da.' responded Jim.

'We got the wee fucker then,' said Joe with a grin resembling that of a Cheshire cat.

'There's no doubt. Now we get his tout bastard da,' he said triumphantly.

Surveillance of the car was easy enough along the Antrim coast road. Joe managing to keep the beetle under control as it travelled along the winding road ensuring to keep it in sight as it went round the never-ending bends. The car stopped in the village of Cushendall. Gina Francis and Paul Tierney exited their vehicle and entered a small café.

Jim felt there was no need to go into the café as it was small and the risk of compromise too great. Although had he entered he may have been able to overhear their conversation but he decided not to risk it. He was adamant he had his man so there was nothing to be gained by exposing himself to the target. *The wee fucker will tell us everything soon enough,* thought Jim.

The young couple could be seen holding hands across the table as they ordered their lunch. Neither of the two men conducting surveillance exited their vehicle but were able to have eyes on the front of the café and the parked VW Beetle. Carlin had managed to take a photo on his phone as Paul was entering the car back at the Ferry Port and had sent it immediately to Declan. He received a very quick one-word response text, "Excellent."

The young couple appeared deep in conversation only pausing to eat their Ulster Fry or as others would jokingly call it "occupied six county fry." Eventually they exited the café only to go into the small Centra store for supplies to last the weekend. Having obtained the necessary goods, they returned to the vehicle.

Carlin noticed that Paul Tierney appeared slightly on edge, looking around the immediate area of the café and Centra store. As he approached the car he once again whilst waiting on Gina to unlock the doors appeared to scan the immediate vicinity. Carlin had to wake up his driver to continue their pursuit of Tierney.

Jim's orders were specific, 'I want you to follow and find out where Tierney was staying and report back the location to me. I also want you to remain in the area but not get to close but rather observe and report. This is one interrogation I have waited over five years for. It's just a pity it's the son and not the father,' Declan had said.

The couple continued their journey up the coast to Ballycastle, eventually arriving at the Sunny Cove caravan park. Joe started to drive into the park when Jim punched him on the side of his shoulder and called him an eejitt.

'I will walk in, it's not like I'm going to miss that yellow Beetle is it,' he said.

'You stay close but out of sight and I will be back once I clock them.'

Jim was able to stand between the laundry and shower block to observe the couple enter their allocated caravan and watched as they settled in. On his return to the car, Joe was once again sleeping in the driver's seat.

'RIP VAN WINKLE,' Jim shouted at him, startling him out of his sleep. 'Let's go, I've seen all I need for now, said Jim.

Chapter 22

Holiday cut short

The door of the single birth caravan was forced open and the two men in balaclavas almost got jammed in the narrow doorway as they simultaneously tried to force their way inside. Paul and Gina were caught completely off guard and tried desperately to free themselves from the entanglement of the bedding. The bed took up all the front of the caravan with its two parallel benches and dropdown table which knitted it all together to form a double bed.

Paul could see there was no escape past the men but he did try to force open the slim front window to crawl out. He was unceremoniously pulled back by his legs but gripped tightly to the window frame in attempt to resist. He was rendered completely winded by the punch to the side of his rib cage. He realised any attempt of escape was futile and the punch soon put way to any resistance or thoughts of an attempt. He tried desperately to reassure Gina who by this stage was in a state of hysterics crying and pleading for the men to stop but it was to be in vain. Paul was dragged from the caravan and thrown into the back of a white ford transit van. Gina was left in its wake at the caravan door uncontrollably crying and calling out his cover name of Peter.

***

Dressed in a set of dark overalls, barefooted with both his ankles and wrists handcuffed to a chair, Paul was cold and frightened. He sensed he was alone in the room but was sure he could hear the crashing of the sea waves and the squawk of birds, *seagulls*, he thought to himself. *He further believed he must be near the coast because he knew from the time held that he hadn't travelled far from the caravan in Ballycastle.*

He was roughed up in the back of the transit van but not badly. Already in his underwear he was forced into the dirty dreary diesel smelling overalls. His hands and feet were bound together behind his back making it impossible to gain any proper movement. Some sort of tape was placed over his mouth and eyes which restricted his breathing dramatically. He felt claustrophobic and struggled for breath only being able to draw shallow breaths through his nose. His minders giving him the odd kick to the midriff whenever he tried adjusting his position on the floor of the van.

***

Investigare

The old cottage outbuilding looked ancient compared to the main dwelling, with its decrepit walls and overgrown roof. The door was ajar and inside, the smell of damp and mould filled the air. A single small window draped with an old hessian sack provided the only source of light. The room was sparsely furnished with a cobweb-covered work bench. The small space was cluttered with tools and equipment for the garden, but in the dim light, it was impossible to make out its details.

The walls were solid brick and would act as soundproofed so that no one outside could hear the harrowing sounds from within. If someone were held hostage here, they would be isolated from the rest of the world, with no escape. The only way out or in was through the door. Overall, the cottage outbuilding was a perfect place to keep someone hostage, keeping them in the dark and out of sight.

The sack was removed from his head followed by the masking tape that had been placed over his eyes. Even in the dimly lit room, he found it hard to adjust to the light causing him to blink several times as his eyes became accustomed to his surroundings. This was not the weekend he had planned or hoped for.

The realisation he had truly mucked up and consequently knowing he had put his family at grave risk. This weighing heavy on his conscience. In the corner of the room sat a rough wooden chair with frayed ropes tied to its legs, seemingly used before as restraints. Paul thought, *what other poor soul had been dealt the summary justice of a so-called court martial by the IRA in this place. He wondered if their crimes resulted in their death and the sentence administered by the same judge, jury, and executioner.*

'Hello Paul, or should I call you Peter? It's been a long time and you've grown so much son,' said the man.

'We need to have a wee chat about your "Tout" bastard da.'

Peter recognised the man as Jim Carlin.

'I have not seen my Da in years, I left home at 17 and went to Dublin to live. We were always moving around from town to town in the south of England. So, I don't even know where they are now, said Peter.' Peter was trying hard to build in some sort of cover story or reason for not knowing the whereabouts of his family.

It was futile and he knew it, but felt he had to try regardless. *It was all about controlled release, blurt everything out and he was dead. There would be no need for them to keep him alive. He had to resist for as long as he could in the hope help would arrive.*

'Good try son, but you were with your da only a few months back. You were down in Manchester watching Celtic and a little birdie tells me you live in Carlisle.'

Peter remembered the encounter with Razor Fox but realised at least they haven't located the family yet if they believed he lived in Carlisle. *Christ my Da will go mad if he finds out I've been coming over here in the first place.*

'I told you; I haven't seen my Ma or Da....' but was interrupted by Jim, 'Let's cut the crap Paul, you're going to tell me where he is or I'm going to hurt you so bad. In the end you

Investigare

will tell all and when you do, I will send your fucking head right to the front door of your house. Do we understand each other?'

Peter never give an answer to Jim but he knew his interrogator never expected one as the message had been heard loud and clear.

'So, are we ready to talk now son?' said Jim.

'I'll tell you shit all, I want to talk to Declan O'Hara,' spluttered Peter.

***

Gina telephoned the police and reported that her boyfriend Paul Tierney had been abducted from a caravan in Ballycastle by two men dressed in dark clothing and wearing balaclavas. She stated he was thrown into the back of a large white van and driven away. Gina was put through to the desk Sergeant of the PSNI station in Coleraine. Between sobbing and fits of hysteria she explained that real name Paul was an Ex-Agent of Special Branch or rather his father Steven was.

***

The telephone rang on the bedside table of Robert "Bobby" Fee the head of TCG (N) Technical Coordination Group (North) at Londonderry. His wife stirred but turned over pulling the quilt of him as she faced the opposite direction. Still half drowsy from sleep he answered the phone and was told the news of the abduction. He immediately got up, putting on his glasses, straining he looked at the digital clock on his bedside table and seen that it was 3:30am.

He swung his legs over the side of the bed and reached down and retrieved his Personal Protection Weapon (PPW) a Walther pistol. Placing his slippers on, he walked slowly toward the bedroom door. The voice from the bed broke into his preoccupied thoughts.

'Everything alright dear?' his wife Ella said.

'Go back to sleep he whispered, I've got to go into the office, I'll speak to you later love,' he replied.

Unfazed Ella turned back pulling the quilt tight against her and went back to sleep. It was nothing new to her, Bobby's job meant him having to go into the office for some sort of crisis at all times of the day and night and Ella was used to it.

Once down the stairs he phoned his duty station officer and enquired as to what stage they were at with the investigation.

'Is he one of ours?' asked Bobby.

'Yes Sir, ex- Sammy Carson's case but it's the son, not the father.'

'Have we got the duty watchkeeper at HQ yet?'

'Yes Sir, he is already on it. MI5 have already started the ball rolling and initiating recontact procedures for their Agents in the hope someone knows something. Our boys are doing the same.'

Investigare

'Good, I'm on my way in but keep me updated,' said Bobby.

***

7:00am, MI5 handlers were already busy telephoning around their Confidential Informants looking for any clues to the whereabouts of Paul Tierney. Instructions were passed for all the Agents to keep their eyes and ears open for any indication or movements by the usual suspects on the MI5 watch list.

***

7:05am. Kathy arrived at the home of the Talbot family having received the call from MI5 Communication Centre informing her that Peter had been kidnapped and she needed to get to the family as quickly as possible. When Kathy received the call she had been working up in the north of the country and operating on another case. This meant she could be at the Talbot's home within the hour minus makeup.

Kathy knocked on the door and watched as Sean walked down the hallway through the small, frosted glass window within the door. She could tell it was him by his gait. He had a very slight limp, this because of a car crash years earlier which shattered his right leg. She wasn't looking forward to what was to follow but clung to the hope that it was some kind of mistake. She waited as Sean opened the door and she could see he was shocked by her appearance.

'What happened, are we compromised?' asked Sean.

'Can I come in Sean? we need to talk.'

'Sorry,' he said, stepping back from the door and indicating she should enter.'

'Of course, please come in.'

As Kathy walked along the hall, she was met by Rita who was standing next to the lounge door dressed in her dressing gown.

'What's going on?' asked Rita.

'Could we go through into the lounge and take a seat?'

Once everyone was seated and perched on the edge of their seats, Kathy gave a small cough then asked.

'Is Peter in his room? yet dreading the answer. She was hoping he was still wrapped up in his quilt fast asleep.

'No, he's with his mate from college,' said Rita.

'Do you have a name or an address for this mate?'

Both Sean and Rita looked at each other and nodded their heads before Sean eventually said, 'No. Christ, I just know that he goes up to Ayr the odd weekend to his mate's house but I have never thought any more about it than that. What the hell is this all about, has something happened to Peter?'

Kathy started to explain to the couple by saying, 'I am deeply sorry but Peter using his alias has been going back to Northern Ireland to visit his girlfriend and we believe he has been abducted by the very people who want you dead.'

'O'Hara the bastard,' said Sean.

Rita let a scream out of her that shook the very foundations of the cottage. It was a long uncontrollable and pitiful shriek.

'He hasn't got a girlfriend in Northern Ireland, Christ he was only a kid when we left,' Sean said.

'I'm afraid that's not true, he had maintained a link to a girl by the name of Gina Francis and had made regular visits to see her.' said Kathy.

Rita having gained a little more composure stated, Gina Francis is only a child,' totally forgetting several years had passed since she had last seen her.

'I know this is difficult but you need to stay calm and be assured that everything possible is being done to locate him as we speak, it's our number one priority.'

'You both need to pack a bag and come with me now as we need to take you to a safe house until we resolve this and get peter back home to you.'

Sean had a million questions to ask but struggled to comprehend the How's, the when's and what on earth made his son to do such a thing, being just a few.

Chapter 23

The Cry for Help

7:30am. Sammy received the call as he just finished his run around the Tollymore forest at the foot of the Mourne mountains near his hometown of Newcastle. He was in the process of making his breakfast which started with three raw eggs in a glass of milk, followed by poached eggs and toast.

'Slow down Sean,' said Sammy,' what's the matter?' 'They've got Peter, the fucking bastards have got Peter.'

'Who Sean? whose got Peter?'

'That fucker O'Hara, that's who.'

'Right Sean, I need you to be calm and explain to me exactly what has happened but I need you to be rational and specific as timing is of the essence here.

Eventually Sean managed to convey what had happened and pleaded with Sammy to do something to help his boy.

'I haven't got long,' said Sean. 'Kathy is here and she's taking us somewhere safe.'

Investigare

'Let me get this straight in my own head,' said Sammy. 'At about 3:00am they took Peter from the caravan park in Ballycastle. The girl was just left in situ, is that correct?'

'Yes,' said Sean.

Sammy then thought, *by his own calculations he has been gone just over the four hours so could still be in transit as they spoke. But then again it would take less than an hour to get someone across the border but the police would be looking for any movement across in that direction. The likelihood would be to conduct the initial interrogation in a safe house prior to any real move away. I don't think any harm will have been done to him yet. Declan wouldn't have been involved in the abduction so his whereabouts at the minute is important. I think "Box" would be concentrating on looking for Peter with helicopter assets and police patrols in the area but without proper details of the vehicle or vehicles involved, it was going to be like looking for a needle in a haystack.*

Sammy then spoke again to Sean, 'Don't be doing anything stupid, leave this to me and I will contact you on this number. One last thing, do you think Peter would have remembered what I said about asking for Declan O'Hara if taken?'

'I don't know, but I hope so,' said Sean.

Sammy ended the call to Sean and then made several calls of his own before getting dressed and leaving the house.

The call for help by Sean and the kidnapping of his lad who would have been about the same age as his own son had he survived the despicable attack by the terrorists give Sammy all the motivation he needed. He may not have been able to save his own son back then but Sammy was determined to save this lad.

***

8:00am, The trip into Belfast took about forty minutes. Sammy arrived in the city to be met by Roy and Davy, his two colleagues. 'Did you manage to get everything we need,' Sammy asked Roy.

'Yeah, we're good to go mate.'

Sammy quickly briefed the team on what had occurred and the need to find Peter.

'Right guys, we need to get over into the west of the city and set up surveillance on O'Hara. We need to be careful because other agencies will be tracking these guys as well. I'll make a few more calls and see what I can find out.'

Chapter 24

I Can't Forget

Through swollen lips and the metallic taste of blood he slowly raised his head. Every fibre of his body ached beyond comprehension. His wrists felt numb from the pain as the circulation was being restricted by the tight binding to the chair. The plastic cuffs had cut into his wrists and ankles with both being red raw.

He had kept his hands clenched in fear his fingers would be removed by the secateurs sitting on the table only a few feet away. The claw hammer which was being brandished in front of him with the continuous threat of having his kneecaps smashed and removed, was becoming more a reality the longer he resisted their interrogation.

The pistol had been placed in his mouth on more than one occasion with its foresight chipping one of his teeth as it was extracted. The last words he heard as the pistol was cocked and placed against his head was, 'Fuck it, I don't believe the tout bastard. Nutt him.'

Sean was thrashing about on the bed, his vest soaked in sweat with tears flowing down his cheeks.

'Sean…Sean, it's all right you were dreaming again, said Rita. Sean took a moment as he set upright stirring at the wall, it had felt so real.

He was back at the IRA safe house being questioned over his part in the botched operation. He did what Sammy had said and denied everything but it didn't stop the beatings or being submerged in a bath full of water.

It had taken a long time to get over that episode in his life but it was back with a vengeance. The Talbot family's life had been turned upside down again. Being placed in a safe house whilst the Security Service, Police and Sammy tried to locate Peter had brought back all the nightmares of the past.

Rita towelled him down and fetched a clean vest for Sean to change into. Once he had calmed down, he turned to Rita and said, 'This can't go on, I need to do something. I can't leave it to the peelers or Box. I need to get home. He is my son and I'm sitting here farting about and those bastards have my boy.' He was welling up again. 'I feel so fucking useless, I need to do this.'

'You can't,' said Rita. 'For one, we couldn't go anywhere as we are being watched by Kathy and others.'

'I never said we, said Sean. 'I could sneak away if you distract them long enough.'

'Sean you would be killed and then what would I do, I will have lost both of you. Leave it to Sammy, he promised us he would find Peter and bring him home. Trust him Sean, trust him. Now lie down and try and get some sleep,' said Rita.

Investigare

Sleep was the last thing Sean could get. He couldn't get it out of his head. He lay in the darkness of the room and contemplated constructing a plan of action. The reality was he had to help his boy.

***

Dressed in two sets of clothes one on top of the other yet hidden under his Rab fleece jacket they left the house for their trip to the local shops. Rita commented, 'it's not that cold outside so why the big jacket?'
'I think I might be coming down with something, maybe it's connected with the hot sweats or the dreams I've been having recently. I don't know,' said Sean.
Sean and Rita were placed in the back of the protection team's car but Sean had to ask Bob the driver to turn the heating down as he was sweating profusely under all his clothing. Once they arrived at the large Tesco store, Sean and Rita were escorted into the store by Kathy. Bob remained outside in the car with eyes on the front entrance. Sean knew it was going to be difficult getting away from Kathy as she seemed to have eyes in the back of her head. Every move he made Kathy seemed to be somewhere in his eyeline. *She seemed to know every advantage point to observe a targe*t, Sean Thought. He remembered how both Kathy and Sammy had given him advice on how to identify if someone was following him. He now wished he had listened better when they discussed how to avoid

or shake off surveillance. He needed to find a way to escape quick, otherwise he would miss his transport links he had planned to use for his getaway.

He left Rita and went to the newspaper counter. Watching his wife continue with the shopping, he could see Kathy watching them both the best she could by positioning herself between the aisles. He was starting to get desperate now. The clothing wasn't helping as he was excessively sweating because of the double layers. *A minute just a minute*, he thought to himself hoping Kathy would drop her guard.

Someone within one of the aisles dropped a glass bottle and the noise of the smash was all the distraction he needed. Kathy had a momentary lapse as she looked round to where the commotion was happening. As soon as her head was turned, Sean bolted for the door and the freedom of the street. He still had to negotiate Bob in the carpark. As luck would have it, a lady was trying to negotiate a food trolly over a small kerb. Sean immediately offered to assist her whether she wanted it or not. It give him the opportunity to sneak past Bob whilst using the lady's body to provide him with cover.

Once past Bob he abandoned the poor woman in the middle of the carpark as he made his way down the street. The bus station was only two hundred yards from the Tesco store. His heart was pounding as he ran half expecting to hear voices behind him screaming for him to stop. The voices never came and he made it all the way to the station without incident.

Once there, he was able to board the bus with minutes to spare before its departure. Having taken a seat at the rear, he removed his jacket and the small empty holdall strapped to his back. He stripped the outer layer of clothes and placed them into the holdall. His anxiety levels were at fever pitch.

As the bus left its stand, he watched out the rear window back in the direction of the store but again he was relieved as there was no sign of his minders.

The bus from Hexham would take him to Newcastle. He felt guilty leaving Rita and hoodwinking Kathy and Bob but it was his boy in danger and he would do anything to get back.

He had made good time getting to Newcastle, transferring to the Metro for the twenty-minute ride to the Airport. Not wanting to raise any suspicions at the house, he had deliberately not booked a flight but believed he could get one at the desk in the airport.

***

Following Sean's escape from the store, Kathy challenged Rita on Sean's intentions and asked if she was implicit in it. Rita stated, 'No, I'm furious, I'm in the dark as much as you, he never discussed it with me. I knew nothing of the plan but I must be stupid because all the tell-tale signs were there this morning.

'Christ's sake, he looked like the Michelin man, all he wants to do is save our boy, but if the IRA don't kill him I will,' said a very worried but petrified Rita.

Kathy had been livid when she discovered Sean had vanished from the shop unnoticed. Kathy knew she had wasted too much time hunting the store for Sean and blamed herself for his escape but still vented her anger at Bob as he was meant to be watching the front entrance, not bloody well reading his gun magazines. Kathy had the embarrassment of having to make several calls reporting his absence.

Rita didn't know what to do for the best. The two girls chatted about how he might travel back to Belfast but she didn't want to betray his trust, knowing what he had previously discussed about going home, but hell, he never even warned her he was going. *I could lie and say he went back to the cottage in Dumfries to buy him a bit of time* she thought. It was a dilemma she really didn't want.

***

Sean arrived at Newcastle airport in Ponteland. The metro stopped at the side of the main entrance to the building. Following a short walk up the ramped walkway, he found himself in a large open spacious hall. The ticket desks were all positioned along one wall to the rear of the hall. He made his way past a large group of Geordie lassies sorting through their bags and preparing for their hen party weekend in Belfast. Something that had become quite popular in recent years as it was both cost effective and considered a popular destination for the night life in the city centre.

He went to the desk of Flybe. The young lady dressed in blue jacket and skirt with a darker shade of blue neck scarf greeted him with a smile and asked if she could be of assistance.

Sean asked for a one-way ticket to Belfast. The young lady informed him the next and last available flight was scheduled for 2030 hours that evening. Handing over £56 he was asked for his name and proof of identification. On handing over his passport, the young lady held it aloft for a second or two as if she was inspecting it before placing it back on the counter.

No sooner had she set it down Sean was approached by two men in plain clothes who spoke his name.

'Mr Talbot would you come with us please,' said one of the men as he picked up the passport of the counter.

'Who the fuck are you,' asked Sean.

'Let's not make a scene Mr Talbot, just come with us for a quiet talk away from the crowds please.'

'You still haven't told me who you are and until you do, I'm not going anywhere with you.'

'We are from Special Branch here in Newcastle and you sir have a very worried wife back in Hexham and she would be delighted to see you back there if you get my meaning. You will not be boarding any flight any time soon, so be a good man and come with us please.'

Sean was removed from the airport to a waiting car. He asked the officers in plain clothes, 'Are you taking me back to Hexham?' The big Geordie Special Branch man said, 'No, I believe a lady called Kathy will be coming to meet you. We are to transport you back to Newcastle and the Northumberland police headquarters to await Kathy's arrival.'

'Christ, she won't be happy with me, will she?' It was more a rhetorical question and not really wanting an answer.

The Geordie responded by saying, 'I think she will just be relieved you are back safe and sound.'

The short journey to the headquarters give Sean time to reflect on his actions. He knew his reunion with Kathy was not going to be pleasant. But it was going to be a walk in the park compared to the wrath he would receive from Rita.

Sean was deliberately left in a cell by Kathy to mull over his actions at Newcastle whilst she spoke with the Special Branch guys, thanking them for their cooperation and apprehension of her man. Following her chat and coffee she asked for Sean to be released back into her safe keeping.

***

The journey back to Hexham was fraught with a mixture of disappointment and despair. Having been read the riot act by Kathy because of his actions, he became subdued. Kathy seeing how dejected he was tried to reassure him that everything possible was being done to find Peter.

Sean whilst on the verge of total breakdown and trying to come to terms with his failure to escape his security service minders, tried to express his feelings to Kathy. It was because she was a woman that he felt he could speak freely and not feel weak as a man who had failed to protect his son. He stated, 'I feel so helpless, what sort of man am I if I can't even protect my nearest and dearest. Those bastards have my boy and I'm here twiddling my thumbs. What sort of dad does that make me!'

Investigare

Kathy found it hard to respond but once again tried to reassure him.

'Sean listen to me very carefully, I know this is difficult, but I promise you we will find him and those bastards you're referring too will get what's coming to them. No stone will be left unturned to root them out and return Peter to you. You have my word on that. You need to prepare yourself now for Rita because she is hopping mad with you. She needs you by her side. She is worried sick at the thought of you doing something silly and taking the law into your own hands. If your ears aren't burning they soon will be, trust me.'

Chapter 25

Ruben

Ruben, the MI5 handler met with his Agent "Thornbush" in the grounds of the Culloden hotel as a matter of urgency to discuss the disappearance of Paul Tierney. The cover name of Peter not being used as a precaution. It was deemed a need-to-know issue and at that time the Agent certainly did not need to know. Thornbush knew about Declan's fixation for finding the Tierney's and stated,

'Declan has made no secret of his desire to hunt him down. His obsession had lasted over five years and his determination in that time has not waned. If anything, it had magnified,' said Thornbush.

Ruben had been Thornbush's handler for four years and during that time Thornbush had continued to provide excellent pre-emptive intelligence that resulted in many drug dealers and dissidents being taken off the streets. The partnership established between the two men had developed into an excellent working relationship with Thornbush believing he was doing the right thing by touting on his so-called friends in the dissidents. Incidents such as the young Dermott Skelly's murder and the impact of the drugs on the other kids in the city making him realise the damage he had been doing in his supplying of drugs in the first place. He desperately wanted Sinn Fein to take action to combat the drug problems.

On several occasions when carrying out his undercover intelligence gathering missions in or around the Sinn Fein offices, he had seen the heartbroken Bobby and Maggie Skelly pleading with Gary McSweeney to take direct action against the drug barons. He knew that their cry for justice was in vain.

Thornbush's involvement with drugs went all the way back to before he was recruited in 1996. He had been employed as a humanitarian aid worker for "Action Against Drugs," a charity which worked in eastern Europe helping drug addict mothers whose babies were addicted on heroin at birth. It was referred to as NAS (Neonatal Abstinence Syndrome). Every drug taken would pass from the mother to her foetus's blood stream during pregnancy, so babies would enter the world addicted and suffering the effects of withdrawal.

Thornbush along with a Scottish friend, Jock McClean, worked together in Albania and got involved with the drugs designed to help ween the addict of their addiction. Working in cooperation with local agencies they found a lucrative market by having access to Methadone the slow-acting opioid agonist. Methadone was provided to the mothers. It was taken orally so that it reached the brain slowly, dampening the "high" that occurred with other routes of administration while preventing withdrawal symptoms. There was ample supply, but they also were able to get their hands on Fentanyl and Heroin.

The temptation became too much for them, so thinking they could make a small fortune, they started to smuggle the drugs back to the UK. They had been doing it very successfully for some time with much of it reaching Northern Ireland.

The trade from Albania to Glasgow using the charity's vehicles had gone undetected for a considerable time. Glasgow had become the drug capital of the United Kingdom, replacing Liverpool following the closure of many of its docks and supply routes.

Thornbush whilst travelling independently back through London's Heathrow airport was stopped by HM Customs officials carrying half a kilo of heroin. Whilst held in a custody suite, he was visited by a plain clothed gentleman who said he worked for the government. He was told he had been observed for some considerable time but that a deal could be done if he was prepared to cooperate by telling him all there was to know about his drug business.

Forensic analysis had been carried out on the white powder and it had the same consistency of that which was flooding the UK market.

After much discussion and the threat of an exceptionally long prison sentence, he decided to come clean and informed on his friend Jock McClean. Thornbush had close connections within PIRA at that time and to whom he had been supplying his drugs. The supply of drugs was deemed a threat to national security with the suppliers in Albania and Scotland having links to PIRA.

Investigare

The drug money was being used for the purchase of weapons to be used by the dissidents in their terrorist campaign, whilst at the same time netting them all nice little holiday homes in the Republic.

It was decided to allow Thornbush to return to Northern Ireland but he was instructed to keep his PIRA connections onside. He was expected to report on PIRA's activities to his new friends from MI5. Thornbush had been a successful Agent for the security service and when Declan O'Hara and his cohorts crossed to the dissidents following the GFA, he was encouraged to follow suit.

***

Jock McClean had served eight years when he was caught coming off the Hull- Rotterdam ferry with five kilos of heroin hidden in several truck exhausts he had used for concealment on his return to the country. His arrest had been courtesy of Thornbush's information. Having served his time, he was now back continuing his drug trafficking on behalf of the dissidents. McClean never suspected Thornbush of his compromise but rather believed it was just down to bad luck. Thornbush was no longer motivated by the threat of prison for his previous demeanours but more to right a wrong.

***

Following the GFA and his release from jail, Declan had been originally employed as a special adviser to the then west Belfast Sinn Fein councillor Gary McSwinney. O'Hara being just another paid convicted terrorist who was getting legitimised or decriminalised with a pay-packet from her majesty's government. As was the case of several others at the time, including Joe Byrne, Jim Carlin, Teagan Greer, and Razor Fox. Positions they eventually relinquished opting for the New IRA and the lucrative drugs market.

Thornbush informed Ruben, 'I've been tasked by Declan to play a part in an upcoming drug deal. A large consignment is expected in from Scotland in a joint deal between several Irish drug dealers and it's to be handed over to a team of dissidents from Dundalk. I've been told it is estimated to be about ten kilograms of heroin.'

He explained, 'a shipment that size would be expected to have a street value of about four million pounds.' He further explained, 'the talk is that it has a purity of about 60%. Considering once diluted it would hit the streets at about 12%.

'By the way, Declan is expected to take receipt of money and a weapon in the village of Carnlough but I don't know from who or how much.'

Ruben was trying to join the dots and believing there could be significance in O'Hara's movements. The proximity of Carnlough to Ballycastle, the fact it was only 26 miles between the two localities and the area of the abduction of young Tierney. Also, because he was taking possession of a gun sent

Investigare

alarm bells ringing in his head. Ruben left the Agent walking around the lavish gardens of the Culloden as he made a telephone call.

Chapter 26

Operation "Quick Fix.

The Scania lorry came down the ramp of the cargo ferry in Belfast docks observed by the E4a surveillance team. The team leader who had "Eyeball" made the call to the rest of the team. 'Standby Standby, X-Ray exiting the port.' The Scania 6x2 wheeled unit capable of transporting a forty-four-ton trailer was today without any legal load or legal cargo. Jock McClean was making his way to Flanaghan's haulage yard in Warrenpoint close to the Irish border. It was there that he was to pick up his load but not before a stop on the outskirts of Newry in the Greenbank Industrial Estate for a drug drop first.

The location had not been conveyed to McClean by his contacts for "OPSEC" operational security reasons. He had been ordered to stop at the services on the M1 and he would be given further instructions. It was all designed to reduce the risk of compromise. The large neon Celtic football badge which usually furnished his cab and could normally be seen in the cab behind the head of the driver had been removed. A precaution McClean had taken purely for the trip to Northern Ireland.

This was a trip which had been done numerous times before. Jock McClean was using a legitimate supply chain in Flanaghan's to illegally import his drugs to the dissidents in province.

The tyres of the lorry made for the perfect hiding place. A quick stop at an abandoned warehouse on the outskirts of Cairnryan, a small village in the historical county of Wigtownshire in Scotland and near the eastern shore of Loch Ryan and the port of Stranraer. It was here that the tyre or tyres would be removed then packed with packets of heroin then re-pressurised and sent on its way. The inner offside tyre on the rear lift-axle would be used believing it would be the most difficult to detect by customs.

As the Scania outbound journey was to be without a trailer, it would mean the inner tyres would remain suspended and off the road ensuring less chance of the heroin packages being damaged or splitting in transit.

***

The Scania unit driven by Jock McClean continued to be followed by the surveillance team from E4a. The Agent reporting on the operation may well have been under the control of MI5 but the powers of arrest and criminal charges were still the responsibility of the PSNI. It was the police who needed to build the case for the CPS (Crown Prosecution Service) to get it to court. Following the De Silva report investigation into the alleged collusion between the security forces and paramilitary groupings, a more coordinated approach and integrated working relationship had been established. The two organisations were to work together to combat terrorist and criminal activity in Northern Ireland.

It was the first such approach to be established in the UK ensuring the whole of the UK had a unified approach in dealing with homeland security. The PSNI would benefit greatly from this joint venture as it would improve their criminal intelligence capability. Operation "Quick Fix" was an example of this in practice.

***

The Scania was followed out of the Belfast docks and tailed as it made its way from the Harbour Road onto the M2 motorway toward the west link. A team from the HMSU was already pre-positioned in the Greenbank Industrial Estate in Newry. Jock McClean made the expected stop at the Applegreen services on the M1 motorway on the outskirts of Lisburn.

Having gone into the building he took a seat and watched for anyone he could identify as potential surveillance who may have followed him in or anyone already positioned in the building. Having satisfied himself he wasn't being tailed; His instructions was to make his way to the toilets. On entry to the restroom, he had line of sight with Thornbush but no interaction or acknowledgement between the two was had.

Thornbush entered the last cubicle and removed the plastic bag which had been placed behind the cistern. Inside the bag was a piece of paper detailing the directions to where the drop off should take place within the Green Bank Industrial Estate. Without having to come together both men left the service station with Thornbush getting into a blue ford escort.

The surveillance team monitored the progress as both vehicles left the services with the escort leading the Scania. The journey down to Newry went without incident with the surveillance team rotating the controlling car.

Once on the outskirts of Newry the call was given to the HMSU team to expect the imminent arrival of the Scania target vehicle. Thornbush made sure to drive slowly as instructed by his handler Ruban.

As he approached the outskirts of Newry, he detonated the small explosive device within the forward roadside tyre completely shredding the tyre in the process and bringing the car to a halt at the side of the road, all of which was observed by Jock in the Scania. Jock could see the blowout and had no option but to follow his instructions and continue to the drop location. This little manoeuvre ensured Jock would arrive alone to the waiting undercover police officers of the HMSU.

McClean reversed his truck down the side road just opposite the Newry and Down Council yard. He parked the truck close to a hedgerow which ran the length of the road and bordered a small no longer operating manufacturing site. His positioning of the truck ensured it was out of sight from the council yard. The two large gates with its chain and mortis padlock secured the site. On the opposite side of the road was a large, galvanised metal fence with barbed wire along the top, making it impossible to breach or climb.

No sooner had he parked the Scania when a white combi VW van with "Haulage Services" displayed on the side entered the road pulling up alongside the Scania. Two occupants dressed in dark blue overalls exited the vehicle and approached McClean.

The Commander of the HMSU team came up on the radio and told his men to wait until he gave the order to effect arrests as he wanted the transfer of drugs to have been completed between both parties.

The occupants of the combi retrieved a wheel complete with inflated tyre from the inside of the van. The commander of the HMSU team was concerned that had they rushed in and effected an arrest without the two Dundalk men being in possession of the drugs then they could have possibly beaten the rap in court, claiming to have been there simply to help in changing a tyre. He wanted them to be in possession of the drugs before giving the strike command.

All three men worked intensely to get the wheel off the truck. As they were in the process of placing it into the back of the combi, the order to strike was given. The flashing lights of the HMSU cars and the shouting from the team concealed within the hedgerow instructing the Dundalk men to stand still took them by complete surprise. It was total chaos for the three drug dealers not knowing where to turn or run. The only exit being blocked off by the cars of HMSU. One of the Dundalk men managed to get to the passenger door of the combi. He reached into the passenger footwell and retrieved a pistol. More shouts of 'Armed police, stand still or I will fire,' was screamed at the drug gang.

The Dundalk man using the cover of his passenger door fired two shots in the direction of the cordon. The response from the HMSU team was quick and decisive. Shots rang out from several of the team peppering the door with tiny holes whilst penetrating the thin metal exterior of the door hitting the man several times in the chest and legs. McClean curled up in a ball under the body of his cab whilst holding his head in his hands in the vain hope any stray rounds wouldn't hit him. The other Dundalk man immediately fell to the ground sprayed eagled offering the team of HMSU no resistance.

The scene was quickly secured and the three men apprehended. Two men were arrested and placed into police cars and taken into custody. The third man was treated at the scene then rushed to the Daisy Hill Hospital for treatment under escort. Despite the best efforts from the ambulance crew, the Dundalk man died of his injuries on route. The police retrieved a pistol along with the 10 kilograms of heroin.

Thornbush eventually arrived near the drop location having replaced his wheel and watched the events unfold from a safe distance as he made a call to Declan informing him of what was occurring and his own predicament of having the misfortune of the blowout. He laid it on thick reporting a gun battle had taken place at the scene with one man being shot and taken to hospital.

Chapter 27

Power Struggle

Since the prominence of Sinn Fein as a serious voice of republicanism, many hard-lined republicans opted for breaking away from the soft line of diplomacy being sought. Criminal activity once controlled by PIRA had seen an increase of factions trying to muscle in on the drug and trafficking trade. INLA and the newly established or regurgitated New IRA were in direct competition for control of various areas in Belfast. Drugs were even being supplied by paramilitaries from the loyalist side of the divide and vice versa.

Seldom were the main players or suppliers ever caught with the drugs as they would use young lads on push bikes to facilitate the delivery of small amounts of heroin to their endless list of addicted customers. The young lads were also manipulated by being paid with drugs which kept them loyal with a level of dependency. These same young lads were being exploited by carrying out the intimidation of would-be debtors of money owed for their drugs.

Investigare

    Control of these areas was hard fought for, with sectarian murders being commonplace. Drug lords were allowed to operate in the areas if the paramilitary groupings got their cut. Declan O'Hara and Co were no different not having to get their hands dirty but reaping the rewards from the ill-gotten gains. The drug problem was endemic.

Chapter 28

Family Matters

Banter Burns and Billy Andrews exited the house and made their way along the dark alleyway back onto the Shankill Road, satisfied in the knowledge that it had been in Banter's words, *a messy punishment beating.* It was one job he was adamant he wanted to conduct himself. Rival drug gangs were carrying out tit for tat attacks and all under the banner of the UDA (Ulster Defence Association). Houses were being attacked with petrol bombs and pipe bombs. Cars belonging to gang members were being torched, all in the bid for control of areas and the leadership of the paramilitary organisation.

The Police and Security Service's intelligence assessment indicated the grouping was at the stage of an all-out feud for supremacy of the drug market in the north and west of the city. The paramilitary group was so fragmented that it had lost all credibility with the local populace. The so-called UDA gangs were deemed by the community as nothing more than criminals' intent on destroying everything that was good. Gang members names were being sprayed on gable walls with warnings of execution if they didn't leave the area. Death threats were commonplace and Stephen "Stitches" McCall was in direct conflict with Burns for control of the lower Shankill. Extrajudicial punishment beatings and shootings had increased by sixty percent since the signing of the Good Friday Agreement in 1998. Neither side of the sectarian divide fully supported the agreement. The Loyalists seen it as very much one sided, whilst the republican dissidents believing it was an appeasement and a sell-out of the arms struggle but claiming it didn't go far enough. In truth, the sectarian groupings from both sides had too much to lose with peace.

Stitches and his men had targeted the most vulnerable in the area, supplying loans that the people couldn't resist but equally couldn't afford to pay back. The terms being impossible to honour with interest doubling every time a payment was missed. They targeted people coming out of welfare offices, drug clinics and benefits offices, then followed them home. Then they would call at the house and offer the occupants money with unrealistic repayment plans. Failure to repay would result in Stitches sending his band of thugs to visit the bad debtors. The mistake Stitches made was sending a team to the home of Banter's nephew.

Retribution was to be swift and life changing. Banter received the call from his dicker (lookout) who had been watching the home of Stitches. Stitches had arrived home from his caravan in Millisle with his wife and two young boys.

Banter along with Billy Andrews went to the house forcing entry through the kitchen door. Stitches was seated at the kitchen table with his family. Billy Andrews rushed Stitches as he was trying to get out of his chair knocking him to the floor.

Banter was standing at the back door having closed it by reaching behind his back and pushing it closed whilst never taking his eyes of Stitches. He then spoke directly to Betty, Stitches wife stating, 'Take the kids up the stairs and stay there until I call you. I want a wee word with your hubby love.'

Betty was furious and shouted, 'Get out of my fucking house you bastards and leave him alone,' whilst holding one of her sons tight against her body.

'If you don't do as I say, I will fucking Nutt him, so I suggest you do as I say and get the fucking kids up the stairs.' shouted Banter.

It was Stitches who spoke next stating, 'Betty love, it's all right, take the kids and do as he said, we will sort this out, everything will be fine. Now go.'

The two young boys were crying and saying, 'Don't hurt my daddy.'

'One of the children ran to Billy and kicked him on the shin shouting, 'Leave my daddy alone.'

Billy let out a cry whilst pushing the kid away and screamed at Betty, 'Get the fucking brats out of here.'

Reluctantly Betty took the boys out as she was instructed, taking them up to the boy's bedroom. She put the boys TV on in their room and turned up the volume to ensure whatever was happening downstairs wasn't going to be heard by the boys. She knew she was powerless.

Back in the kitchen, Stitches was put back into the chair with Andrews placing a strap around his waist thus securing him to the chair. He was still able to move his upper body and head forward but was restricted backwards as his back was up tight to the back of the chair.

'Listen here you little shit,' said Banter to Stitches.

'How fucking dare you go after one of my family and break one of his legs. You left him in a terrible state.'

'I didn't know he was related to you, but he owed me money,' said Stitches.

Banter removed a black gas canister normally found inside a fire extinguisher from his jacket and hit Stitches across the head causing a large gash above his right eye.

The area around his eye immediately started to swell up closing his eye.

Banter then took hold of Stitches right hand and placed it on the table, holding it tight by the wrist, he then smashed down hard on the hand breaking several of his fingers. The cry of pain would have been clearly heard up the stairs such was the intensity of noise. There was no explanation needed or wanted, it was just a reprisal attack for his nephew. By this stage there was no resistance as his head was laying forward with his chin on his chest. Andrews grabbed Stitches hair from the back of his head and banged it down hard on the table almost toppling the chair in the process.

Stitches appeared to be unconscious or was pretending in the hope of avoiding any further punishment. However, Andrews lifted Stitches left hand placing it on the table and taking a kitchen knife from its rack stabbed into the hand impaling it to the table. Stitches cried out in pain but it was Banter who had taken hold of Stitches wrist and pulled his hand back away from the table and in doing so ripped the hand through the knife splitting through the flesh and fingers. Blood was running across the kitchen table in a crimson flow mixing with the dishes still in place from the family meal.

A few more thumps with the gas piping to the head and body of Stitches rendered him slumped to the floor still attached to the chair.

With a final parting of words to the semi-conscious man to get the fuck out of the area or be nutted whilst swaying a 9mm browning pistol in his face. They then left the house back into the alleyway and made good their escape.

Chapter 29

Fear and Suspicion

Teresa believed Marie was still having a challenging time settling back into normal life following her incarceration. Their relationship was becoming strained. Teresa didn't like the fact Marie would continue to go out on her own late at night. At first Teresa was suspicious that Marie was dating someone as she was always very vague about her absences. She thought Marie was being so secretive because it was a married man.

Teresa tried to ask her friend on several occasions about where she went, but Marie always seemed to dodge the question with a smile and was quick to change the subject. Teresa couldn't help but worry as the whole disappearing act made her uncomfortable.

She decided to try and have it out with Marie as this was one of the rare occasions when Marie was not heading out but rather had stated she was going to have a bath and an early night. Marie had filled the bath adding bubble bath and lighting several scented candles to complete the ambient environment she craved. Teresa waited until Marie was in the bath and relaxing before entering the bathroom and sitting on the toilet seat next to the bath then stated, 'Marie love, I need to talk with you and I don't want it to become a problem between us but I need you to be honest with me.'

'Not another bloody inquisition,' said Marie. She continued, I can't leave this bloody house without you wanting to know where I'm going, who I'm going to see, or when will I be back. Christ, I may as well be back in prison. You're worse than those friggin prison wardens.

'I'm sorry, said Teresa but I need to discuss this.'

'Christ's sake, discuss what,' said Marie as she raised herself more upright in the bath.

'It's just that we've had some what I can only describe as slightly disturbing conversations and combined with your absences at night I'm struggling with it, said Teresa.

'What's so disturbing Teresa,' Marie said getting increasingly irater by the minute.

'Well for one, you told me that Ted Bundy picked up a degree in psychology before he entered law school and it was there he learnt one of his many ruses from his psychology experiments. You studied both those subjects in prison.'

Marie laughed and said, 'are you being serious?'

'It's not funny Marie, to make a comparison such as Ted Bundy gave me sleepless nights.' Teresa was shaking inside and she could feel her anxiety starting to creep up to almost fever pitch as she was about to come out and ask her next question.

'Marie, when Teagan Greer, and Razor Fox, were murdered, they were in the IRA at the time of your husband's murder. You swore vengeance and I was there at court remember, when you said you would get all those responsible for his death,' said Teresa.

Teresa could see she had upset Marie with her line of questioning but she needed answers.

'Teresa, do you really think I had anything to do with those bastards murders?' Listen, if you live by the sword then you should die by the sword. Look, I'm delighted to see their demise but I had nothing to do with it.'

'Yes, but you talked about how satisfying revenge is and used the example of Marianne Bachmeier who became famous in Germany after she shot and killed the murderer of her seven-year-old daughter during his trial in a courthouse in Lubeck.'

Teresa thought about it for a moment, *what Marie did to her husband's killer was horrific so maybe she was capable.* Teresa then tried desperately to construct a timeline for Marie's movements. Teresa had no idea what Marie got up to when she was at work. Marie did go out on several evenings never telling Teresa where she was going or who she was meeting. So, she guessed anything was possible. Marie's excursions at night had almost become regimented in the timings and frequency.

Not knowing the connection between Marie and Bap Quinn, meant Teresa was at a lost as to why she would have killed him. He wasn't one of the ex-PIRA members responsible for the death of her husband, or so she thought. She could understand the motive to have Razor Fox and Teagan Greer killed but not Bap. Although he wouldn't be missed and as far as Teresa was concerned, good riddance to bad news.

Teresa watched as Marie had to add more hot water to heat the bath and could see she had forced the point a little too hard. As she got up to leave the bathroom Marie said, 'Teresa the reason I talked about Ted Bundy and Bachmeier was because they were case studies I had to do for my degree. Now listen, I don't want to talk about it anymore. I just want to soak and chill.'

As Teresa got to the bathroom door, Marie said, 'Teresa I think I should look for some place of my own. Its time I moved on in my life. I've been thinking about it and I'm meeting someone tomorrow to look at a few properties which would give both you and I our own space.'

Teresa lied by saying, 'There is no rush to find somewhere, I enjoy having you here.' However, Teresa was happy Marie was looking some place to live as she was worried by her comings and goings and what she perceived as dark conversations. Teresa wasn't buying her explanations. There were just too many coincidences with people being killed and them having some sort of history with Marie. Teresa did have the tendency to over analyse things or at least that's what she told herself. Whatever the circumstances she would be pleased to have her place back to herself again.

Chapter 30

The Take-away

The car left Sandy's bar and made its way out onto the M2 motorway. Declan was being driven by Micky Finn. The team from the E4a police surveillance unit were monitoring the movements of both men and vehicle. The initial trigger away from the pub was done by an operator on foot as holding down the position in a vehicle would have been extremely difficult.

The area was tightly controlled by "dickers" or kids simply known as lookouts employed by the main players. Young lads or girls would be positioned on street corners with the sole purpose of watching for strangers, "The men in the cars," the latter referring to surveillance teams.

'Standby Standby, that's Tango1 and Tango 2 complete the X-Ray (car) and mobile toward you Echo1.'

'Roger, I have control,' came the response from the mobile callsign.

Sammy and his team remained well back not wanting to get mixed up in the follow or chase as the police would describe it. Sammy was reliant on Fred at DDT to keep him informed of the whereabouts of Declan and Co.

The surveillance team followed the target into the Applegreen services on the M2. The vehicle pulled in at the petrol pumps but no one alighted from it. A two-man team of E4a had followed the car into the services with the other two vehicles involved continuing past, taking layup positions at the next slip road at the Templepatrick exit.

Declan (Tango1) exited the vehicle, wearing a dark green Helly Hansen fleece jacket and paddy cap. He was observed by the team entering the building via the southern door but the driver (Tango 2) still made no attempt to exit the vehicle. It appeared strange to the team as no petrol was being put into the car yet they were taking up a fuel pump bay.

A debate was had between the two surveillance operators as to the level of risk if they were to follow Declan into the building. But as luck had it, a minibus full of adults pulled into the forecourt and made their way to the main entrance. It was judged the group of men would provide excellent cover for an operator to blend into as they made their way toward the building, thus making it hard for Tango 2 to pick out surveillance, if as the surveillance team had expected, Micky would be watching Declan's back.

'Standby, Standby,' came the call, 'That's X-Ray mobile toward the side of the building and the east exit.' After a brief silence, the radio burst back into life.

'Tango 1 out through the east door and is going complete in X-Ray with Tango 2.' The operator inside the building questioned the call stating, 'Are you sure it's him? because I

Investigare

thought I caught a glimpse of target heading toward the toilet area.'

'Yes, get back to the car, target has already been picked up.' The surveillance team relayed their calls but allowed the target car to proceed without immediately following it out of the services. Acknowledgement was received by the two supporting cars knowing they would have a visual soon enough. Once several other cars had exited the services the surveillance car slotted in behind them, using them as cover then re-joined the chase.

***

Sammy who had used the cover of the small minibus to enter the services, took up a position with overwatch of the immediate area. This ensured he remained out of sight from the E4a surveillance team. He scanned the area of the carpark and watched as the surveillance car exited the services. The call from Fred at DDT provided Sammy with live updates of the terrorists' phone activity and positioning. Sammy was informed that the phone of Declan O'Hara was still stationary at the Applegreen services.

Sammy was joined by Roy and Davy at the services but avoided coming together opting to remain on comms but within eyeline with each other.

Roy went into the building and identified Declan who was seated at the far end of the eating area and adjacent to Burger

King. Roy sent Sammy a SITREP, (Situation Report), then took up a seat covering both exits.

He observed Declan who had just completed his own deception by swapping positions with another ASU member in identical clothing and of similar height and build.

Sammy made a telephone call stating that whoever was in the car with Finn, it was not Declan O'Hara. He listened to the response then laughed and said into the handset, 'Because I'm looking at him now.' Then the call was ended.

**

Declan watched Finn exit the Applegreen services along with his decoy replacement, being delighted that his deception plan had worked. He also observed the surveillance team's car pick up the operator who had followed Declan into the building and follow Finn. This gave Declan a profound sense of satisfaction.

Once both parties were clear of the services, Declan made a call to Finn telling him to take a nice long drive and visit the Junction One shopping centre in Antrim ensuring he kept the bastards busy but not to react. Now that he believed he had lost the surveillance it was onto phase two of his plan. He had planned to make a quick stop at Carnlough for a money drug and weapon exchange before heading to Ballycastle to deal with that wee fucker Tierney.

Investigare

***

Earlier that morning, Sammy had been called and had a conversation about an intended meeting in Carnlough which O'Hara was expected at. It was reported that O'Hara was meeting someone at the Glenhope bar. When Sammy had briefed his team he stated 'Change of plan lads, we are going to keep a close watch on this one as Declan is expected at Carnlough today for some sort of meeting. There may be teams of surveillance on him and the door kickers of HMSU will probably be in close support.'

***

Declan having waited a good fifteen minutes decided it was time to go. Having picked up a burger and drink from Burger King, he made his way outside. Placing his hand inside the bag containing the burger he withdrew the keys to the Honda Accord. The young lad in Burger King played his part well and made for a good custodian of the keys. He would be well rewarded later with his free fix of heroin or a few quid.

Declan left the services closely followed by the team. He made his way to Templepatrick then cut across country to Ballyclare and out the Shillanavogy Road to Carnlough. It was not the ideal road to conduct surveillance on as it give several opportunities for what a surveillance operator would term "A long look back" potentially highlighting any following cars.

It was fortunate that the team knew or at least believed they knew O'Hara's intended destination. Also having his telephone tracked helped by allowing the team to keep its distance.

Once in the village of Carnlough, O'Hara visited the small post office located beside the stone harbour and arch. This being a main feature of the village which was first constructed in 1854 by the Marquess Marchioness of Londonderry.

Being first on the scene, Roy set up an observation post (OP) so that he could observe Declan drive into the carpark. He observed Declan O'Hara drive in and park up next to a black BMW 3 Series. He watched as another individual got out of the BMW and go to the boot of his car. The two men exchanged small black holdalls.

A large heavyset bold man in his early forties got back into the black BMW. Being comfortably concealed in his OP, Roy observed and recorded both men's actions. Both men's cars were hidden from view of the main road and appeared to be out of sight of any CCTV. It took a second or two for it to register but Roy now thought he recognised the heavy-set bloke.

'Standby, standby,' came the call from Roy as the two men entered their respective cars. 'That's Tango1 entering the vehicle. Wait,…. Tango 2, Christ it's Banter Burns,' reported Roy.

The radio fell silent for a second before Sammy responded, 'Banter Burns the fucking Loyalist?'

'I know no other,' answered Roy.

Investigare

'Declan O'Hara and Banter Burns, Holy God, that's some cross community project taking place,' Sammy said sarcastically.

'Roger,' came the response by Davy. The next call from Roy was informing the team that O'Hara and Burns were mobile in their respective cars toward the exit and the main street.

Davy was next to radio the location of the Honda Accord as it turned left toward Cushendall. Burns in his BMW turned back in the direction of Belfast. Sammy and Davy had boxed off the carpark ensuring whichever way O'Hara's car exited, it could be triggered through their position and the follow could be undertaken without reacting to the move. Sammy who was located outside the Post office on main street was able to observe the Accord travel under the old stone archway at the harbour as it passed his location, followed loosely by Davy.

Roy hastily extracted from his OP and made his way back to his car to get into the pursuit of O'Hara. The car travelled along the Antrim coast loosely followed by the team, each taking it in turn to be lead vehicle. The changeover of the controlling vehicle took place at each of the small villages on route, Waterfoot, Cushendall, and Cushendun. This ensured the changeover of vehicles seemed as natural an occurrence as possible.

The follow was routine procedure for the team and they encountered no issues during the journey up the coast. Sammy was the lead vehicle when the car exited the village of Cushendall and headed north in the direction of Ballycastle.

Shortly after leaving Cushendall the Accord was joined by a black Peugeot 208. Sammy came up on the radio and stated,

'All callsigns be aware we have a black Peugeot 208 now fronting the Accord.' Davy and Roy knew this would be Declan's guide and protection for the remainder of the journey.

Sammy's mobile pinged and the message he received stated three telephones were in frequent dialogue. Declan O'Hara, Jim Carlin, and Joe Byrne. The phone rang, this time it was Fred from DDT. He stated, 'Be careful, Jim Carlin's phone is about eight hundred meters ahead of you. You could be driving into trouble. It appears he has come together with O'Hara.' Sammy let Fred finish before stating, 'He's escorting O'Hara in a Peugeot.'

Sammy then paused and realised what Fred had just said. 'Eight hundred meters ahead of you,'… 'Wait, are you tracking me as well,' asked Sammy, with a sarcastic laugh.

'Christ, I need something to make the task worthwhile and anyway, I want to keep you boys out of trouble,' Fred said with a chuckle.

'Seriously Sammy, be careful, I had located Carlin's number earlier and he appeared to be somewhere near Ballyvoy toward the coast. I was hoping to get you use of satellite. Big Duncan at OSS (Optimum Satellite Services) has promised to help if he can, so standby for update.' However, Duncan has already stated, there appears to be a weather front coming in of the Atlantic, so the cloud cover may hamper his efforts. 'Thanks Fred, I owe you one,' said Sammy.

'Isn't that what you said the last time?'

'Ok two,' laughed Sammy.

Sammy conveyed to the team what he had received by text message and his talk with Fred. The cars continued out the

Investigare

Cushendall Road through Ballypatrick townland before the Peugeot led the Accord off the main road toward the coast.

Davy was the lead car and radioed the change in direction stating, 'That's O'Hara turning right onto Murlock Road, I'm not going to follow him down and risk being compromised.' The small sign at the turning read, "Sir Roger Casement Memorial." Sammy thought, *it's ironic they would be in that area* as *Sir Roger Casement was an Irish diplomat and republican leader who was executed by the British for his part in the easter uprising of 1916.*

It was decided that Roy would commit down the road at least as far as the memorial as he had the least exposure to the target during the morning. Sammy and Davy continued to Ballyvoy and encountered an PSNI checkpoint on the main road checking cars. A quick exchange of pleasantries with the officers soon seen Sammy and Roy through the checkpoint and on to a suitable layup position in which to park the cars.

A quick change into a more suitable attire for the terrain was then completed. HK53 assault rifles with retractable butts made for the perfect weapon and fitted neatly into their backpacks. Both men also had their own Personal Protection Weapon obtained from their time out in Iraq and not traceable back to them. The two men set off on foot over the rugged and bleak terrain in pursuit of the target. The satellite telephones each of the lads had would prove to be invaluable as the telephone signal in the Glens and surrounding coastline were terrible.

Roy had a spectacular viewpoint from the wooden cross at the memorial. From its elevated position he had breath taking views of the Antrim coastline and the rugged green pastures of the countryside.

The area was deserted except for a male and female hiker in matching dayglow yellow hiking jackets and walking aids. Their small day packs had silver water bottles dangling from the straps. The bottles casting reflective rays of light as the last of the afternoon sun hit them. It was like some kind of SOS distress signal.

Roy had passed the Accord which was parked in a dilapidated cottage and had been hidden behind the building. It was only because of the freshly created tyre tracks into the site that Roy even noticed the car.

***

Having hidden the car, Carlin transferred Declan into the Peugeot then took him to his destination.

Roy an ex-member of the Special Operations Group and surveillance expert had no trouble in following or locating the Accord. He relayed its location over the radio to Sammy and Davy. He then got himself into a position to observe the small cottage which had the Peugeot parked in its yard.

Chapter 31

The End Game

The hessian sack was abruptly removed from his head. The brightness from the single light bulb hurt his already swollen eyes. He had soiled himself but it was out of desperation and being tied to a chair for a prolonged period, rather than fear. There was no other light in the small outhouse other than when the stable door of the shed was opened and closed. The small window with its hessian sack offered nothing in way of light. So, it was impossible to say what time of day or night it was most of the time.

He didn't recognise the voice that was talking to him now, but it was different from the one who had been torturing him thus far. *Is it really torture he thought.* He hadn't been badly beaten It was more sleep deprivation that he suffered from. *Then again that is a form of torture,* he concluded. His captives were wearing him down, getting him ready for the real deal and now the man in front of him was probably the one to do the real damage. At least he hoped that it was Declan O'Hara otherwise he would probably never see the outside world again. As he opened his eyes wide and as he adjusted to the light, he was focused on the door but there was no one there to rescue him.

'Hello wee man, do you remember me?' said Declan. Paul slowly lifted his head and looked up at Declan who was standing directly in front of him, arms across his body with a large smile spread across his face.

'It's been a long time and you have grown so much. It doesn't seem like yesterday you were running around our streets with snotters running down your face. Now look at you, all grown up and the image of your da. Oh, how is he by the way?' It was rhetorical rather than a question as he wasn't expecting an answer.

'Now here's the thing,' but before he could continue Peter's head dropped down again. 'Hay wee man, look at me.' said the man in front of him.

'Do you know who I am.'

Fuck I'm being tortured by someone who doesn't know who he is, he thought sarcastically.

'Sorry I can't help you there, maybe one of your monkeys could help you out with that one. 'Although he tried to speak without fear, his voice had a shakiness about it and it give him away as he sounded nervous.

Declan O'Hara let a laugh out of him and said, 'You're a cocky little fucker aren't you Paul.'

Paul never gave any form of response selecting to ignore the comment directed at him.

'I'll tell you this for nothing, you have more balls than your da, I will give you that much. Now here's the thing. I have travelled all the way up here and in case you're thinking the boys in black are going to turn up and save you, then you are sadly mistaken. They're too busy shopping in Antrim,' he said with a chuckle.

'This won't take very long. So, you are going to tell me where your fucking da is and I'm not going to hurt you. This doesn't have to get nasty. Just tell me the whereabouts of your da and I will let you go. It is a simple arrangement. If you don't tell me, then my friend Jim here is going to do you some serious damage and you will become another statistic. It is what we in the IRA call the "disappeared." You will never be found. Your ma, bless her, will not have a grave to visit. Oh, and by the way wee Gina sends her love. So, you see its simple really. Where is your fuckin da?'

Paul tried to play it straight, trying hard not to give anything away, but when Declan mentioned that he would go and have a wee word with the lovely Gina, Paul's body language told a different story. He could see Declan had picked up on his concerns. He shifted in his seat, squeezed his hands into tight fists which only added to his discomfort as the straps around his wrists dug deeper into his already sore and raw skin. Paul didn't know what had happened to Gina when he was abducted but he was sure she was still at the caravan. Reality was, for all he knew, she could be next door in the cottage.

Declan addressed the lad again, 'Paul this isn't IRA business anymore, this is personal and that means I will stop at nothing or anyone to get my answers, including your wee girlfriend, Gina. Keeping silent is not going to help you it's just putting you one step closer to the grave. Your silence is admirable son, but as the Italians would say, "Omerta" is indeed honourable but unlike the godfather movies, it will still get you killed. Declan continued to play mind games with Paul. He had decided to use psychological warfare on the lad.

The threat of torture being his main avenue of attack. He really didn't want to hurt the lad and had stated at one point that it was the "Sins of the Father" and nothing to do with the lad. However, to gain what he needed then he wouldn't hesitate to harm him.

Declan continued to ask Paul as to the whereabouts of his da but Paul was being obtuse and giving nothing away. Like a scene from the Reservoir Dogs, Declan was whistling a tune as he slowly walked back to a table and the black holdall on it from which he took out a claw hammer.

He ambled back across the room to where Paul was still strapped to the chair. Without breaking his stride and continuing to hum an unrecognisable tune, he lashed out with the hammer, smashing it into Paul's right kneecap. The sound of the bone shattering and the cry of pain reverberated around the shed. Declan stood back and watched as Paul tried desperately to regain some sort of composure.

Paul, dizzy and feeling nauseous from the blow threw up what little he still had in his stomach. He had seen the hammer in the hand of Declan as he approached but the speed in which he smashed it into his knee took him by complete surprise.

Declan stepped back within striking distance again. Paul hands had been stretched out over the end of the arms of the chair. His fingers expose but gripping the end in the hope of warding against the excruciating pain he was now experiencing.

Seeing Declan step back toward him he immediately clenched his fists fearing the next blow would be into the hands busting his fingers.

Declan stood over him and exposing the claw end of the hammer whilst grinning a menacing smile and said,

'I'm going to rip out that fucking kneecap unless you start fuckin talking boy.'

Paul, once again looked toward the door whilst silently praying for help to arrive. He wasn't prepared for this and knew he would eventually talk. Everyone talks in the end. That's what his Da had told him when he asked about people who had been abducted by the IRA. It was not like he could invent reasons for not blabbering out the location of his family indefinitely. He was tired, hungry, and in so much pain. He just wanted it to stop before he would end up being crippled for life, or worse, buried in an unmarked grave.

Declan deciding to have a bit of fun, walked back to the table and his little bag of tricks and placed the hammer down. He then turned toward Paul and said, 'Step up to the Oche.' Then he produced a set of darts and threw one at Paul hitting him in the chest. Paul let a yell out of him as the dart penetrated the boiler suit and his chest. 'I call that a twenty, I wonder if I could get a double top. No maybe not, I haven't had enough fun yet.'

Without warning he threw another dart hitting Paul on the shoulder which received the same reaction but more in anticipation of pain rather than actual hurt, but this time the dart bounced off the body landing on the floor. 'The next one will be right between the eyes if you don't start talking son,' said Declan.

Declan then threw another dart, this time at his bare foot hitting him on his big toe. Once again Paul let out a scream but was unable to move his foot as his ankles were secured to the leg of the chair by plastic straps.

Declan let out a big belly laugh, then turned to Jim Carlin and said, 'I think it's time we got serious here. This wee lad thinks we're mucking about. We're going to finish this now and then I'm going to go and pay wee Gina a visit.' Declan nodded to Carlin who moved over to the side of the room and picked up a Jerry Can and brought it to the rear of Paul's chair. He then bent down to retrieve the dart still embedded in Paul's big toe. He twisted it before withdrawing it. Once again, Paul let out a gut retching howl.

The hessian sack was placed back over his head. Paul struggled but it was in vain. I guess you are dehydrated so let me put that right. Carlin pulled Paul's head back as O'Hara lifted the twenty litre can and started to pour water over the face of Paul.

Paul coughed and spluttered as the contents which smelt and tasted of petrol was penetrating his nose and mouth. It was water but the previous contents of the can must have had petrol in it prior to Carlin filling it. Paul struggled to breathe as he was being water boarded. O'Hara kept repeating the torture method until all the water from the can had been used. Paul was once again retching and gasping for breath as the hessian sack was pulled from his head. The fumes and taste of the contaminated water resulted in Paul vomiting again.

Investigare

'Now here's the thing Paul, that was just a form of refreshment. Had I decided to properly waterboard you, then I guarantee you would suffer unimaginable pain. You would suffer a physical and psychological sensation like that of drowning such as you just experienced but I would do it at a much slower pace and trust me when I say that is real torture. To have a single drip dropped on you would feel like a simple tingle hitting your forehead but over time it would become a feeling of utter anguish. You would beg me to cut your head off because it would become so unbearable. Eventually you would completely lose your mind. But here's the thing, I think pain and suffering should be administered at a good pace. It should be unpleasant or else where is the fun in it.'

'Are you ready for a wee chat yet son?' asked O'Hara. Without waiting on a response, he continued, 'I swear to God son, I will cut of every one of your friggin fingers and if you persist in not telling me where your da is, then I will cut out your tongue and you will disappear. At the end of the day, I will find your da with or without you. So be smart and let's end this now. Tell me where your ma and da are and you can go on with your life with wee Gina and have lots of good catholic babies together. What do you say? I will give you a few minutes to think it over.' O'Hara handed over the 9mm pistol from his waistband to Carlin then walked to the door before turning back and said, 'Look after the wee man, I'll be back after a have a wee chat with the lovely Gina.' Reverting to his psychological ploy. He then exited the shed leaving the door ajar.

Paul knew he couldn't withstand much more and just wanted it to end. He was ready to confess all, when Carlin walked over to him and punched Paul full on the face breaking his nose. His face became a bloody mess. The force of the blow tumbled the chair backwards with Paul landing on his back on the floor but still secured to the chair. Carlin was standing over the top of him looking down at Paul and stated, 'Now I get to have my fun.'

As Paul tried to recover from the punch and fall he could see stars in front of his eyes but it was a red spot that got his attention. It was on the rafter of the building. He became captivated by it as it seemed to move down the wall of the shed before disappearing behind the back of Jim Carlin.

The sound of something landing on the floor and rolling across the room had Carlin turn back toward the door. Simultaneously the stun grenade exploded as the weapon laser finder found the centre of Jim Carlin's chest. This was followed by the sound of the dull crack from the HK53 automatic rifle. Carlin fell backward spinning from the impact landing face down directly in line with Paul's eyes. Although dead, his eyes were wide open and staring directly at Paul. The sight of Davy in the doorway brought on an uncontrollable surge of emotion from Paul with tears flowing down his face.

'You're safe now son, it's over, I'm a friend of Sammy's and we're here to get you home.'

'Is Gina okay?' Paul asked through tears.

'Gina is safe, she's not here so don't worry.'

***

Forty-five minutes earlier the team of three men had met at the monument. Davy briefed the team on his observations and the positioning of Declan O'Hara's car which was some two hundred meters to their south in a ruin. A damp dreary dull mist had rolled in off the Atlantic reducing their visibility whilst clouding over what had been an otherwise cool crisp dry day.

Following a quick set of Quick Battle Orders by Sammy, the three men checked their weapons and equipment. Once they were happy the three men tracked across the fields to the cottage. As the men crawled into position with overwatch of the cottage they observed a white transit van and a black Peugeot parked in the yard.

Three men were sighted at the cottage. Jim Carlin, Joe Byrne, and Declan O'Hara. They observed as the men moved about the small yard between the cottage and outbuilding. Sammy tasked Roy to do a quick CTR, (Close Target Recce) to the rear of the cottage looking for any windows or openings to the outbuilding. Roy noted two windows one of which was frosted and believed to be the bathroom. It only had a small rectangle opening at the top and therefore was considered by Roy to be too small to climb through. The other being a bedroom window on the gable wall.

Knowing the gable wall and its window could be covered by Roy from the front of the property, it was decided that a frontal assault would be needed to gain access into the building. Unless all three of the gang were co-located together in the cottage, it would come with the added risk of Paul being in the line of fire in the outbuilding. Otherwise, it would need to be a concurrent breach of both the cottage and the outbuilding to achieve the element of surprise.

The door to the cottage was open and from their advantage point could see clearly into the open doorway and the kitchen. The outbuilding had a stable door which was open. The team watched as Declan O'Hara left the outbuilding and went into the cottage. He couldn't be seen as he went through the kitchen toward the rear of the property.

The mist had brought with it a slight drizzle and therefore made it less likely of engaging any of the gang in the open yard. Sammy decided he would go into the cottage and take out Declan whilst Davy did a frontal assault on the outbuilding. Roy was tasked with providing cover support to the two men. However, from Roy's position he could see Joe seated at the kitchen table. It was decided Roy would engage Joe once Sammy got into position adjacent to the entrance. This would enable Sammy to concentrate on the breach and the taking out of Declan.

Each of the team now had their own target to neutralise. It needed to be coordinated to enable a quick assault and maintain the element of surprise. Everyone would act on Davy's stun grenade exploding after it had been thrown into the outbuilding. Roy would then take out Joe seated at the kitchen table. As Declan was unsighted, he would need to be found by Sammy conducting a room-to-room search.

On hearing the stun grenade go off, Joe jumped up out of his chair. Roy who already had his sights locked onto his target, opened fire with a single round hitting Joe squarely in the forehead sending him back into the chair, with his body falling backwards, landing against the aga range cooker. Sammy was already moving at speed in through the entrance in his pursuit of Declan firing a round into the body of Joe for good measure as he passed. Roy made his way down the slope to help Sammy in his pursuit of Declan. The sudden sound of breaking glass was heard by Sammy to the rear of the property.

Sammy shouted into the radio that O'Hara was making good his escape through a window at the rear. On arrival in the bathroom Sammy could see a wooden laundry basket had been used by Declan to break the window. Blood was evident on the shards of broken glass still protruding out of the window frame. Sammy could see O'Hara running across the rough open countryside in the direction of the coastal path.

Taking aim, Sammy fired a single shot in the direction of O'Hara but never appeared to have found his target. Sammy knew he only had a small window of opportunity as Declan would be out of sight and hidden in the rolling mist if he didn't get a move on.

He came up on the radio again stating, 'Going on foot in pursuit.'

'Roger, Sammy, you're going on foot, I will back you,' came the response from Roy.

'Negative, secure the place and clean up' said Sammy as he made his way over the coarse grass in pursuit.

'Roger said Davy,' acknowledging the radio chatter and commands. 'Target down and the lads safe,' was the next call received from Davy.

Sammy was gaining on O'Hara but he was still too far ahead to get a good shot. The pursuit wasn't helped by the undulating ground and the poor visibility. Every now and then he would lose sight of his target and then suddenly the target's head would appear again just above the horizon. They twisted and turned over the land before eventually finding the hiking tracks or moreover trampled grassed walkways used by the hikers. This enabled quicker movement along the coastline.

The chase eventually ended at Fair Head, one of the great headlands of Ireland. A magnificent sight and one that could be seen from the Mull of Kintyre in Scotland on a cloudless day. The massive basaltic cliff fell sheer for one hundred and eighty metres with some of the columns being fifteen metres wide and hundreds of metres high. The whole area was steeped in myth and legend, including The Grey Man's Path, the Grey Man being a spectre that is supposed to be seen when the mist rolls in from the sea and it takes a human form up the gully.

This was one occasion when Sammy didn't feel like the grey man he had always prided himself to be. Always in the shadows fitting into the background and not standing out. He was no longer in his usual covert mode but found a profound sense of irony being alone at this magnificent landmark with a terrorist who had caused so much pain and suffering.

Having run out of land to run, O'Hara had stopped, turned, and faced his hunter.

Panting for breath and with his hands on his knees crouched over, O'Hara lifted his head and looking directly at Sammy asked, 'Who the fuck are you?'

'Your worst nightmare, that's who,' answered Sammy.

'You couldn't just leave it alone could you. You're an evil piece of work. That young lad has never done anything to you but you and your vengeance holds no bounds does it.' Sammy stated this without expecting an answer.

'Who the fuck are you?' O'Hara asked again.

'I'm the last person you will ever see on this earth. I'm a friend of Steven who is angry with you threatening him and his family. Well, it ends today, Declan.'

O'Hara desperately tried to figure out what had taken place here. *Had Tierney hired a hit team, because he had heard no formal warnings or shouts of "Police" back at the cottage. Then again, could it be an undercover SAS team tasked by MI5 to carry out its dirty war,* he thought.

Looking around for some sort of escape route, O'Hara now realised he had nowhere to go. Directly behind him was the large rock formation of the Grey Man and the deep ravine beneath it. He contemplated trying to cross the narrow ledge knowing he would be in the sights of his pursuer's gun. Then again, he had nothing to lose. He managed to get to one side of the rock formation, briefly being hidden from view, but Sammy was quick to respond to O'Hara's movements.

O'Hara managed to get onto the cross section of the ledge but in his haste to get away lost his footing on the slippery surface because of a mixture of moss and alga. Sammy was quick to catch up with him as he was still prone on the ledge. Sammy kicked out at O'Hara placing a boot into the centre of his chest. The impact sent O'Hara toward the edge with him just managing to grip a small crevice within the rock edge. His legs fell away from his body before coming crashing back into the rock face. They were now dangling over the edge with only his hands saving him from the fall into the ravine and certain death.

He was unable to pull himself up onto the ledge. He pleaded with Sammy to help him.

'Listen, I have a holdall of money in the boot of my car and it can be all yours. There's £50,000 in it, and I swear Tierney has nothing to worry about anymore. I'll never go after him again, I swear it. The lad never talked, so it's over, I swear it.'

Sammy smiled and moved toward the edge of the ledge surface and the petrified looking Declan O'Hara. Looking around to ensure no unsuspecting hikers or tourists were nearby, Sammy took a step forward and with his size nine boot stood on the left hand of O'Hara, crushing the phalanges of his hand. As he twisted his foot from left to right on top of his hand, it sounded like the crushing of spices in a pestle and mortar.

The screech from O'Hara reverberated all around with the echo travelling up the ravine sounding like a ghostly wail. Having had his hand crushed under foot, he was left dangling with one hand but was losing any grip that he still had.

Sammy crouched down beside O'Hara and pulled back one finger, snapping it in the process. This was enough for O'Hara to lose what control he had left and plummeted from the ledge. Sammy watched the fear in his eyes and sense of desperation as he fell in what seemed slow motion to the bottom of the ravine smashing his body on the rocks below.

Investigare

***

The cottage and outbuilding had been cleaned up by the team. It was clear that Paul wouldn't be able to walk out of there with the damaged done to his knee. He was not released by the team from his restraints of the chair but was given something to drink. It was important he remained exactly where he was until the arrival of the police and emergency services. It was to look like a rival drug gang had carried out the executions. 'If you are asked if you had seen or heard anything, then over the commotion of the gunfire and shouting, the name Banter may have been overheard,' said Sammy. A confused but compliant Paul Tierney nodded his understanding.

'You're safe now son, I promised your mum and dad I would save you. I'm only sorry we couldn't get to you sooner. The lad started crying again but it was from shear relief as he said thank you to the three men.

The police would find Declan's car but eventually they would also find his body if it hadn't been washed out to sea. The car would be burnt out. Peter was told by Sammy just to relax and wait for the police to turn up as they would arrange to get him home. They had ensured the body of Carlin was placed away from the outbuilding. A pistol had been recovered from the dead criminal, *a 9mm pistol and probably the one that had been supplied to banter for the killing of Sniffer Horan,* thought Sammy. The same pistol O'Hara had taken back earlier in

Camlough from Burns. He was told to tell the police he was in the outbuilding with the doors closed and was too frightened to make any noise in case he was discovered by whoever was doing the shooting. The small amount of blood in the outbuilding would be assumed to have been Paul's from his beatings, Paul was still in a state of shock but was reassured that he was safe now.

Sammy made a call on his sat phone before leaving the cottage. The team made their way to the car of Declan O'Hara. Having broken into the vehicle and retrieved the black holdall with its £50,000 and two kilos of heroin, the vehicle was set on fire. Sammy and Davy then crossed the prairie grass landscape in the late afternoon drizzle. Roy had made his way back to his car at the monument to ensure he was far away before the police showed up. Sammy and Davy lay in watch from their makeshift observation post and observed as the police arrived followed by the fire service and ambulance. The plume of smoke from the burning car drifted into the air mixing with the damp mist.

Having been satisfied by what they were witnessing, and knowing that Peter was now safe, they withdrew from their hidey-hole and made their way across country back out to the main road and their cars. It was time to become invisible again.

Investigare

***

Kathy had received the call from Sammy informing her of the whereabouts of young Paul Tierney. She immediately contacted MI5 at its Belfast office and spoke with Ruben. The official version choreographed by Kathy was that Thornbush had passed the information as to the locality of the cottage, having been requested by Declan to come and help. Kathy knew Ruben would play along with the deception. Thornbush would be none the wiser as to the Intelligence report being submitted onto the secret terminal at Ruben's office accredited to him.

Ruben, Kathy's long-term boyfriend was responsible for contacting her in the first place following his meeting with Thornbush at the Culloden. Kathy in turn passed on the information to Sammy. The numerous texts received concerning telephone numbers being used and any intercepts were being passed by Kathy to Sammy directly as she received them.

Memories run long and emotions deep. The shooting of Ruben's cousin, Rupert Conan Smythe by O'Hara needed avenging despite the passage of time. Ruben had thought about it for a long time and remembered the quote from his studies of Shakespeare: *Vengeance is in my heart, death is in my hand, blood and revenge are hammering in my head.*

He now had his revenge and Declan O'Hara was just another statistic of the drugs and criminal scene in Northern Ireland. Karma has no menu, you just get served what you deserve and as Declan O'Hara had done, he lived by the sword, so he died by the sword. He would not be missed. There was always someone else ready and willing to step up and take over in the supplying of drugs, extortion, and human trafficking. Micky Finn was now one step closer to achieving his aim.

Two days after the drug gangs' demise and following an anonymous call from a female caller. Detective Sergeant Ken Stones and his team arrived at the home of Banter Burns on the Shankill Road. His home was searched and a small quantity of drugs seized. The search then moved to the BMW 3 Series parked outside the home. Recovered from the boot of the car was a black holdall containing £20,000, two kilos of heroin and a 9mm browning pistol. Burns DNA was found on the holdall having handled it in Carnlough and although the pistol was clean, Ken Stones was confident that once the pistol came back from ballistics there would be a match for the murder weapon used to kill "Sniffer" Horan and Dermott Skelly.

A young mother pushing a pram at the time of the Skelly murder had already identified a person matching Burns description. The £20,000 would have been deemed to be the payment for the contract killing of Horan.

The three men watching the events unfold from the bottom of the road had a satisfying grin on their faces as they watched Banter Burns being led away in handcuffs pleading his innocence stating he had been set up. He was about to be interviewed by one of the country's best interviewers. Knowing Ken Stones, the way Sammy did, he knew the detective would use every trick in the book to get under the skin of his detainee and more importantly, get the confession.

Investigare

Having given each other a clap on the back for the excellent CME (Covert Method of Entry) which they had conducted the previous evening into Banter's car. They turned their vehicle and headed back into the city centre for a well-earned meal. When they arrived at the restaurant, Ruben and Kathy were already in situ and waiting their arrival. Sammy's phone buzzed with the sound of the text message coming through. The message read: "Enjoy your meal folks. Sammy laughed aloud and shared the message with the others as he read aloud his response. "Stop tracking me Fred." Each of the people present looked at each other with a questioning expression on their faces as if they could also be getting tracked by Fred. All deciding to switch off their phones before laughing and raising their glasses and saying, 'Cheers Fred'

Chapter 32

The Walk In

The walk to the Springfield Road police station was a sombre one which was not helped by the unexpected rain fall that evening. Once again Barney got it wrong on the NITV forecast. It was a miserable night, extremely dark due to the heavy clouds lingering over Belfast. The stranger believed after tonight it wouldn't matter as the only daylight or sunshine to be had would be from behind iron bars in prison.

The stranger pressed the button on the small metal intercom box. The sound of a high pitch tone penetrated the night air before being answered by the duty police officer. The stranger was asked to move slightly to their right so as they could be in view of the camera on the intercom box.

Once stood in the correct position the officer at the other end of the intercom system said, 'Good evening, how can I help you?'

'I would like to speak with someone from serious crime please.'

'Can I ask what it is in relation to?' asked the officer.

Investigare

'I would prefer it if you would open the goddam gate and let me in first. It is throwing it down here and I'm getting soaked,' said the stranger.

'Sorry, yes of course, wait for the buzzer and then push the door. You will be met just inside,' said the apologetic officer.

On entry to the station the stranger was met by another officer who asked if there was anything on their person that could cause injury or deemed to be threatening or dangerous to the officer prior to a body search taking place.

The stranger removed a large boning knife from their jacket and stated. 'You will find this is the murder weapon used in the killings of Teagan Greer, Razor Fox, and Bap Quinn.'

As the stranger was in possession of an offensive weapon the officer was obliged to immediately caution the stranger before being taken to a small interview room and offering a hot drink. The Stranger was told that a DC (Detective Constable) would be along shortly to conduct an interview.

The DC arrived a few minutes later and having determined the background and seriousness to the stranger's presence, left the interview room and made a telephone call to Musgrave Street requesting someone from the CID come to Springfield Road to collect said individual for interview as it was a suspected multiple homicide case.

The stranger was stripped and instructed to dress in a set of overalls which were provided. The clothes were bagged for forensic analysis.

***

It took twenty minutes for DS Ken Stones to arrive at Springfield Road Police station and enter the interview room. Ken was well known and respected in the force and the city. With over twenty years' experience working the streets and investigating serious crime.

His colleagues used to say he could get a confession out of a dead man. He had noticed a notable change over the years with extortion, trafficking and drugs being the main causes of crime now. Back in the day, it had all been sectarian and religiously driven but not now. This was a real murder investigation and something he relished as an investigator. He had hoped when he was told for the need to get across to the Springfield Road station it was some kind of mix up and the person being held was not as he had been informed. Taking an intake of breath, he entered the interview suite.

'Good evening, Mr Skelly, or can I still call you Bobby?' Bobby Skelly simply nodded at the officer. I'm so disappointed to see you here. You've gone and got yourself into a right mess. I had hoped you would have left this to the police to deal with.'

'I couldn't just sit back and wait. Those bastards needed taken out and even if you had managed to arrest them, they would have gotten away with it with their fancy republican lawyers, said Bobby.'

Investigare

DS Stones looked disappointed and reluctantly started the interview process. 'I believe you have the weapon allegedly used in the murders of Teagan Greer, Razor Fox, and Bap Quinn. Would you like to tell me how you came to be in possession of this weapon Bobby.'

'Well, I don't have it anymore, one of your colleagues has it,' said Bobby Skelly and it's not allegedly, it is the murder weapon and the reason I know it's the murder weapon is because I used it on all three of those bastards.'

Having admitted to the murders, Bobby Skelly was reminded of the caution he had received and asked if there was anyone he wished to call, maybe a solicitor, suggested Ken. He refused the opportunity to make a call. He was told he would be taken to Musgrave Street where he would be held and formally interviewed. Within the half hour Bobby Skelly was in the back of a police car and taken to Musgrave Street.

On arrival at the serious crimes' unit, Skelly was booked in by the custody Sergeant and briefed on the terms in which he was being held.

A murder investigation was launched by CID. A Senior Investigation Officer was brought in to oversee the case.

Skelly having already been stripped for forensic evidence was placed in the holding cell whilst a team led by DS Stones went out to the Skelly home to conduct a search of the property for any items of forensic value that could be used in the case.

DS Stones having complied with all the relevant codes of conduct was able to formally arrest Skelly and get a special sitting of court the following morning. Skelly was charged with three separate counts of murder. It was important everything was done to the letter as the Judge in charge of the case would ask the case officer, DS Stones if he could connect the suspect to the charges against him. Stones would convey to the judge that he could and therefore would expect the accused to be placed on remand pending his next court appearance, which would be his trial.

When DS Stones conducted the interview of Bobby Skelly under caution, Skelly was unrepentant for his actions outlining in detail his movements and subsequent murders of the three individuals.

He explained, 'Following the death of my son Dermott at the hands of the drug gangs, my wife Maggie suffered a complete mental breakdown and never recovered from the loss, she became a shadow of the woman I had married and loved.

She was put on anti-depressants and would never leave the house. She would just sit there mourning the loss of our boy. They didn't just murder my boy that day, they killed my wife. She sits in the house in a vegetative state. She never missed me out of the house as I went about hunting them down.

They robbed us of the one precious thing we had in our lives. They deserved to die for what they had done. We tried to get justice by speaking to Sinn Fein and that useless idiot McSweeney, but they did nothing. They knew who those people were and did nothing about it. Too busy lining their own pockets I guess.'

Bobby Skelly held nothing back making the case against him rock solid. DS Stones never had an easier case to solve.

Skelly went into overdrive by explaining his actions.

'I had been conducting my own surveillance on O'Hara but he always had people around him making it harder to achieve a suitable time and place in which to carry out my plan. I managed to follow him over several weeks and I nearly got caught in the crossfire when someone took a pot shot at him coming out of Brenda's Café late one night. It was one of the few occasions he was out on his own. I also thought I had managed to follow him out to Antrim and the Junction One retail park but somehow he managed to disappear. I watched as undercover Police cars boxed in his car but it wasn't him in it.'

With an intake of breath and a long drink of water he continued. 'I know a loyalist drug lord had fired the shots that killed my son but all the others were just as guilty. I hadn't given up hope of getting revenge on the loyalist but had found my attempts of pursuing him more complicated hanging around the Shankill Road and I couldn't go into any of the bars he drank in. Maybe if I had interrogated my victims prior to killing them, then I may have got what was needed, but patients is a virtue and something I don't possess.'

Ken not wanting to interrupt Bobby's confession took notes so he could go back over the details with him to clarify any points later. But Bobby was doing a great job at condemning himself.

Ken eventually managed to ask about the meticulous way he went about the pursuit of the three men he did kill. He found it intriguing that Bobby could have left no evidence at any of the crime scenes. Ken knew the weapon used was a boning knife but never made the connection to Skelly and him being a butcher.

Bobby explained, 'My skill as a butcher, give me an exceptional ability to handle a boning knife with precision and efficiency. With each strike of the boning knife, I could leave no room for error. I also have a good understanding of the human body and how to manoeuvre the knife in a way that would cause minimal bloodshed.'

Bobby said, 'My one regret was the death of the lady in the bed. Her death was regrettable but it was because of the struggle I had with Bap Quinn. The gun went off during our struggle, killing the poor woman. As far as the other three, they were all Malign bastards and deserved to die.'

Skelly told Ken Stones that he had Bap Quinn in his sights and it was almost perfect. 'I watched Quinn come out of the Shamrock, a known republican den on Balken Street. He was alone and I thought, *I got you, you bastard.* He turned into an alleyway to the rear of the pub which I thought was strange but believed he must have got cut short and needed to relieve himself. I closed in on him but as I had reached the entrance to the alleyway, I could hear a female voice and it was the barmaid who had come out the back of the bar for a shag. So naturally, I decided not to go in for the kill as she could have raised the alarm very quickly and I may not have gotten away. Anyway, I didn't want the wee girl to witness it. But in the end another female died when I killed him anyway.'

'Why did you hand yourself in Bobby,' asked a bewildered Ken Stones.

Investigare

'When I heard you had arrested Banter Burns and the news broke about the death of O'Hara and Co, I had no good reason to go on. I figured, I've no Son to leave the business too and if I sell, then the money could go to looking after Maggie.

***

The news of the arrest and subsequent charges against Bobby Skelly sent shockwaves around the community. But none more so than in the household of Teresa Coyle. She always had Marie down as the prime suspect. Although not wanting to believe it but the evidence was stacked against her. All those late-night excursions and talk of vengeance. The vagueness as to what she was up to, combined with the stories of Ted Bundy and Marianne Bachmeier really did have Teresa convinced. *Christ what a relief*, Teresa thought. It was the one real reason it was stopping her committing to a meaningful relationship with Marie.

Now that the news had broken, she set down with Marie and confessed her suspicions over the previous month's nocturnal absences from the house.

'I know what you told me the last time but that night in Sandy's when you asked to leave early, I found it strange and it seemed to happen immediately after Kevin Moore entered the bar,' said Teresa

'Did you expect me to sit there and drink with one of the men who I believed may have been responsible for my husband's death? really Teresa, did you? said Marie.

'No, maybe not, but it was the way you went out of the house again as soon as we got home. I did not know what to think and then they all started getting murdered. I felt like I was getting disinformation by your actions as if some sort of deception was taking place.'

Marie laughed aloud. 'Christ Teresa. Your quoting T.S Eliot's poem Gerontion.' Who? said Teresa.

'Wilderness of Mirrors, it is a metaphor for disinformation in spy fiction. I have not misled you. You saw what you wanted to see. That night changed me in a way I could never have expected. I really did have a headache and I walked in the hope of shaking it off. I sat down on a bench next to St Mary's chapel when a couple came across and asked me if I needed any help. They offered me a blanket and a cup of tea. Jesus Teresa, they thought I was homeless. I know it was dark but Jesus did they really think I was that destitute. As it was, they were street pastors out late at night looking to help the homeless.'

'I don't get it Marie; you were out a lot more than that one night.'

'I know. The thing is, we got talking and one thing led to another and I ended up going to a small mission hall and spent the next two hours preparing tea and talking to homeless people. Having spoken to the pastors, they thought I could help these people who had fallen on challenging times and most through no fault of their own. Most of these poor souls were just victims of circumstance.'

Investigare

The pastors worked for an organisation called "Helping Hands" and I've been adopted as their unofficial legal adviser. It's doing simple things like filling in paperwork for housing applications or assistance with benefit claims and such like.'

Both girls laughed at the ridiculous nature of the suspicions held by Teresa.

'God Teresa, I have lost ten years of my life and I am grateful to Bobby Skelly for getting rid of those scum bags but that poor man will spend the rest of his life behind bars and must live with what he had done. I've been there and I wouldn't wish it on anybody. I lost a good man in my husband. As I said before, these parasites live by the sword so they should die by the sword. I will not lose any sleep over them.' Both girls embraced with Teresa whispering into Marie's ear. 'I'm sorry love.'

Chapter 33

New Beginnings

Thornbush drove his car into the grounds of the Culloden hotel and parked next to the black Audi A4. He got out of his vehicle and climbed into the passenger seat of the Audi. 'Hello Kevin, it's been a remarkably busy and interesting few weeks. Did you make sure you weren't followed.' asked Ruben, despite knowing Thornbush was meticulous in his tradecraft. Parked away from any prying eyes or ears in a secluded corner of the hotel carpark, Ruben conducted his debrief of Kevin Moore. His contribution being commended by Ruben, having provided the much-needed information that brought about a phenomenally successful drugs bust against the dissidents. His information concerning O'Hara's movements also enabled Sammy and his team to conduct an effective strike and rescue mission of Paul Tierney. A generous bonus would be paid to Moore for his contribution.

If Agent Thornbush thought he could rest on his laurels he was sadly mistaken. Ruben passed a folder across to Kevin, and

Investigare

the Agent quickly scanned through the contents, nodding in agreement as they discussed the details.

'Remember, discretion is key, and your security is paramount,' the handler reminded the Agent. 'The success of this task depends on your ability to blend in and not draw attention to yourself.'

The Agent nodded again, committed to memory the details of what he had just read and the various cover stories he would use to avoid detection.

As they finished their coffee from the flask Ruben had produced during the debrief, Ruben reminded the Agent of the importance of staying in communication and reporting any updates or changes to the plan.

The Agent left the handlers car returning to his own before exiting the grounds of the Culloden Hotel, blending back into traffic on the crowded Bangor Road toward Belfast to begin his latest mission, confident in his newfound self-assurance and ability knowing he had brought down several leading members of the New IRA. He chuckled to himself as he contemplated MI5's latest person of interest, Micky Finn.

***

Bobby Skelly was escorted from his cell to the interview room and his visitor. Ken Stones thought Skelly was holding up quite well following his arrest and charges of murder. The two men set facing each other with a cup of coffee in their white polystyrene cups, DS Stones updated Bobby on the most recent events concerning the deaths of three dissidents, knowing that Bobby would take solace knowing the intimate details particularly if it concerned O'Hara and Burns. Ken explained O'Hara's twisted and busted body was found at the bottom of a ravine. The other two having been killed by suspected rival drug gangs. It appeared O'Hara had tried to run from the gang and fell as he made his escape.

'There is a God,' said Bobby to Ken as he looked toward the ceiling. Bobby Skelly admitted he would never get over the death of his son. He was still tormented by the vision of his wife Maggie that day cradling the head of their dead boy. He took some comfort from the fact that all of those involved had received their just reward for their actions. Although even death seemed too good a punishment for them.

***

Marie had continued her work at the refuge centre for "Helping Hands" and had begun a relationship with one of the street pastors. She continued to stay with Teresa at least for now. Marie and Teresa came to an understanding that although they enjoyed each other's company and the odd fumble under the bed covers, it would never be a committed relationship as they both would still prefer a relationship with someone from the opposite sex.

Chapter 34

Some months later

The Talbot family had been reunited. Kathy brought Peter back to Dumfries having spent several weeks in Musgrave Park hospital in the military wing having several operations and a new knee replacement. Peter was delighted to be back home although scarred but was trying to put the ordeal behind him.

The nightmares he had been having were becoming less frequent. Peter had been able to telephone Gina whilst in Musgrave but the kidnapping had the profound and overwhelming effect with Gina wanting to end the relationship fearing she could be targeted now that their affair had become public knowledge. Peter was upset but knew his actions could have cost his parents their lives. So, he accepted the breakup.

He was now enjoying lazy days back along the riverbanks of the Nith river and the fierce competition for the biggest catch. Sean was just relieved that as a family they had come through the ordeal relevantly unscathed, undetected, and safe from Declan O'Hara.

***

Sean and Peter sat frozen and unsure of what to do. They could feel their hearts pounding in their chests as the figure got closer and closer. As the sun was behind the figure and shining directly into their eyes, it was impossible to make out who or what it was.

They had never encountered anyone else on this stretch of water the whole time they had fished it. As the figure got closer to them, Sean and Peter could finally make out the silhouette of a man. A man dressed entirely in black, with a long coat and hat that obscured his face. He was carrying a dark black object in his right hand, As the man got even closer Sean feared the worst.

'Christ not again,' he said aloud. Half expecting the man to raise what Sean thought must have been a weapon. He knew there was no hope of escape, Was this how his life was to end? All he could do was reach out taking hold of Peter's arm and brace himself for his death.

'Do you mind if I join you?' Sammy said, placing the small fishing rod in its black canvas holdall on the ground.

'Christ Sammy, you scared the living daylights out of the two of us there.'

'Sorry boys, Rita told me where you were and its definitely fish and chips for supper.' Sean and Peter embraced Sammy both being mighty relieved and delighted to see the man who had saved them. The three men had an afternoon of fishing

Investigare

but still had to visit the fish and chip shop for their supper. Sammy telling the two men he was useless at catching fish but was better at catching bad men. I guess I should be known as a "Fisher of Men."

THE END

Epilogue

An Afghan Bride

'Take cover,' was the shout from the gate sentry at Green Village, a private contractor's compound in the east of Kabul. The Ex Gurkha-soldier turned back toward the advancing truck laden with its five-hundred-pound bomb. Raising his rifle and taking aim through his iron sight ensuring it was aligned on the driver. The ex-soldier could see the white of the eyes of the Taliban suicide bomber as he steered his instrument of death directly at the gate.

With a shout of "Allah Akbar" he crashed through the main entrance detonating his deadly load. No sooner had the sentry shouted his warning when the thunderous noise of the explosion rocked the very foundations of the compound. The shock wave from the kinetic force produced by the explosion shattered the windows of the converted shipping containers used by the Afghans for their bazaar shops, showering the occupants with fragments of glass. The impact of the truck demolished the front entrance but was halted within the chicane which had been designed specifically for the purpose of channelling or stopping such a breach. The detonation managed to blow in the inner gate thus compromising the internal security of the compound.

The six personnel on duty never stood a chance as the ball of fire rose high into the sky turning into a gigantic black cloud of smoke and debris which descended as a dark blanketed mass covering the compound and temporary blocking out the sun. The force of the blast catapulted the Ex-Gurkha-soldier hired to protect the dignitaries within into the blast wall killing him instantly.

The carnage caused by the truck laden with its lethal cargo left a 25-metre crater in the ground. Sammy was settling into his new surroundings having just landed at Hamid Karzai International Airport a few hours earlier. The explosion knocked him of his feet as he was putting away his clothes into his wooden wardrobe which landed on top of him.

Shaking himself free and wrestling with the pile of shirts he had just manage to place on hangers, he grabbed his rifle and body armour and immediately ran for the corridor. He was quickly joined by other contractors as they quickly made their way to the entrance of the building.

'Welcome to Afghanistan,' came a voice behind him.
'The shelters fifty meters to the left another voice shouted.'

The sound of Kalashnikovs could be heard as the compound security were exchanging gunfire with the twenty Taliban fighters now rushing in the exposed entrance. Sammy turned right and away from the safety of the shelter opting to help defend the compound from the would-be attackers, believing the best form of defence was attack.

He ran past the recreation building and Gym with its over turned sports equipment crushing glass beneath his feet as he ran. Suddenly he was knocked of his feet with the sudden impact of a grenade exploding to his right. Twisting his body into the prone fire position he brought his rifle up to the aim whilst looking over the sight and barrel in search for a target or targets.

A Taliban fighter armed with an AK47 was closing in quickly on him. He was instantly recognisable being dressed in typical Afghan 'perahan tunban' (Baggy top and bottoms) with a turban. Sammy took aim and with his rifle on semi-automatic mode fired a short burst of 2-3 rounds hitting the fighter in the centre of his chest rig. One of the rounds ricocheted of the magazines within the rig and struck the fighter in the throat with the other rounds penetrating his rig and chest cavity.

The fighter fell to his knees with his arms dangling by his side as if he were getting ready to start to pray to Allah. Sammy was transfixed on the body in front of him still in the upright position but clearly dead.

People don't die kneeling up except in the movies, thought Sammy.

The shout of 'Target right' and a volley of shots brought Sammy back to his senses and he instinctively rolled out of the prone position he had previously adopted to seek a more secure

Investigare

and somewhere that could provide both cover from view and fire. He found it in the form of a small fountain and water feature located in the small communal gardens next to the dining facility.

'Go firm Sammy the Guardian Angels have it now.' As Sammy looked up, members of the Blackwater Security Company were running pass but already the sound of gunfire had started to diminish. The man's voice Sammy had heard was now standing next to him.

'Are you going to lie there all day or can we get a beer.'

Sammy looked up at the face in front of him, 'Davy…good god, I didn't know you were out here!'

'It's my second-year mate, welcome to New Discovery.'

Printed in Great Britain
by Amazon